PROFESSOR FAIRWEATHER HITS THE SKIDS

PROFESSOR FAIRWEATHER HITS THE SKIDS

A Novel in Stories

BY

JIM STORY

Blue Mile Books, 2025.

Publisher's Cataloging-in-Publication Data
(Provided by Cassidy Cataloguing Services, Inc.)
Names: Story, Jim, 1936- author.
Title: Professor Fairweather hits the skids : a novel in stories / by Jim Story.
Description: [New York, New York] : Blue Mile Books, [2025]
Identifiers: ISBN: 978-0-9862382-4-6 (paperback) | 978-0-9862382-5-3
(ebook) |
LCCN: 2024926270
Subjects: LCSH: College teachers--Employment--Fiction.
| Poor--New York (State)--New York--
Fiction. | Job hunting--Fiction. | Nineteen seventies-
-Fiction. | New York (N.Y.)--Economic
conditions--20th century--Fiction. | LCGFT: Short
stories. | Humorous fiction. | BISAC:
FICTION / Literary. | FICTION / Humorous /
General. | FICTION / Short Stories.
Classification: LCC: PS3619.T67 P76 2025 | DDC: 813/.6--dc23

FIC0000000 FICTION / General
FIC019000 FICTION / Literary
FIC016000 FICTION / Humorous / General
FIC029000 FICTION / Short Stories (single author)

This book may be purchased in bulk for promotional, educational,
or business use. Please contact your local bookseller or the
publisher by email to Bluemilebooks@gmail.com .

Paperback ISBN: 978-0-9862382-4-6
eBook ISBN: 978-0-9862382-5-3

Library of Congress Control Number: 2024926270
(in case you need that, too)

BISAC: FICTION / Literary. | FICTION / Humorous
/ General. | FICTION / Short Stories.

Classification: LCC: PS3619.T67 P76 2025 | DDC: 813/.6--dc23

For Ron Story, Laura Ricard,
and of course, my darling Jill

The 1970s were a difficult time in New York City—poverty, crime, blackouts, riots, stagflation, insults ("FORD TO CITY: DROP DEAD!")—and difficult for more layers of people than one might suppose.

Contents

A NEW REALITY DAWNS

WHEN HE RECEIVED his last payroll check from Brooklyn Quintessential University at the end of the summer, Robert Fairweather's first thought was to immediately apply for Unemployment. Thank God he lived in the United States and not some impoverished third-world country! Imagine what some poor fellow in India or Thailand would be undergoing in a similar situation; how hopeless that would be!

He remained confident that he'd eventually find a position at another university or college somewhere in New York or New England (so his own department chairman had assured him!) but since that hadn't yet happened despite his many overtures throughout the summer and even earlier, he figured: Let's just be sensible here and apply now. It therefore came as quite a shock when the pleasant and apologetic fifty-year old man with thinning brown hair at the applications window informed him that his *particular* university, which he'd had no prior reason to doubt was a right-thinking and responsible institution, had *never* made the required payments into the unemployment coffers. Therefore, *none* of its laid-off employees—whether professors, electricians, janitors, or people who washed dishes in the cafeteria—was eligible. The university had never signed up for it. Never bought in . . .

Robert was aware they were a private university, of course, but who knew they were even allowed to do that?

A few weeks later, no position he was remotely qualified for having appeared, despite his increasingly desperate poring over the Employment section of *The New York Times*, aware that his available funds were about to become only a fond memory, he admitted to himself that Welfare was now his only option.

The gentleman that he finally got a chance to speak to at the Welfare Office—after he'd taken a number and sat for most of an hour—was a very pleasant-looking man named Kanti Patel. He smiled warmly at Robert as he welcomed him into his office, rounding his desk to take Robert's proffered hand in both of his and grasp it firmly.

"I'm here to apply for welfare," Robert said.

"Of course," said Mr. Patel. Reseating himself, he slipped a form out of a file folder on his desk, grabbed his pen, and working from the form, began asking the apparently customary questions.

"How long have you been out of a job, Mr. Fairweather?"

"Well, I was let go from BQU at the end of the spring

semester and I've been trying ever since—actually, I started even before that, of course—from the moment I realized I had been let go . . ."

"Yes, yes! How terrible! That must have been awful! A dreadful experience, to be let go from a job like that! You were a teacher, I presume?"

"Uh, yes, I was. I taught Russian history. No one was more shocked than I when I discovered they were not only laying off faculty, but—'guess what, Dr. Fairweather!—you are to be among them.' Not unlike having someone place his hands on you in a game of tag and shouting, 'you're it!'"

"How dreadful! So, have you filed for unemployment?"

"Of course! I filed immediately, but . . . it appears my university did not pay into the system. Therefore, I'm not eligible."

Mr. Patel, whose brows were contorted with a sense of the unfairness of Robert's tale, shook his head sadly. "Terrible. Just terrible. Okay, then. Allow me to get from you some personal information."

After a few moments of transferring Robert's answers to the form, he asked, "I assume you have no money in any bank, right? No savings?"

"Well, not much, certainly. I've so far only managed to keep a frightfully meager amount in my savings account. I'm down to my last $67."

Mr. Patel's pen stopped moving. A woeful look came over his face.

"You're saying you have a bank account? With $67 in it?"

"Why, yes! In that bank right across the street. Citizens First National, I think it's called. That's a good thing, is it not? I apologize that it's such a paltry sum but . . ."

"Oh dear, Mr. Fairweather. That won't do at all. To go on welfare, you have to be broke. You have to have nothing."

Robert looked at him in shock. "You mean I can't even *apply* now, when I'm down to my last sixty-seven bucks? I certainly can't pay my rent with that! And it's due! I still have to eat, too, you know? It's, it's... habit-forming."

Mr. Patel looked crestfallen but shook his head. "I'm sorry. Requirements are that you must be penniless, I'm afraid. You must have nothing. Zero. I believe the favored American expression is: zilch." He opened his hands, spreading them wide. "I'm sorry."

Robert sighed, looked out the window and shook his head. Then he said, "So, what would you recommend I do?"

"The only thing I can suggest, Mr. Fairweather . . ." He took a moment to look at his watch. ". . . is to draw out that $67. You have about fifteen minutes before 3:00. Close your account and come back to me but . . . in a week's time. Unfortunately, not a moment before. When you are able to honestly swear you are penniless, I will sign you up."

Robert shook his head sadly and rose from his chair.

"Then that's what I'll do," he said. "If I must, I must. Mr. Patel, may I ask for you when I return?"

"Of course. I'll need to take my clients in the order of their arrival, to be sure, but you may most certainly ask for me."

Two weeks later, although he had closed his savings account and then applied for welfare, as Mr. Patel suggested, he'd yet to receive a check (he was told there'd be a three-week delay), his rent had still not been paid, and he had received a notice that the building's managing agent was about to initiate eviction proceedings. Robert swore when he saw that notice in the mail. "These apartment buildings are owned by the university, for God's sake! Fuck's sake, guys! First you fire me, for no good reasons I can see, next you deny me unemployment insurance because you don't pay into the system, now you're trying to evict me? How fucking heartless can you get?"

Once his rage had dampened from a boil to a simmer, he considered what he should do. Well, he needed a lawyer, didn't he? To advise him of his next move? He didn't know any but he'd noticed on a recent walk to Brooklyn Heights that there was an office on Court Street (a ten-minute stroll from his apartment building) that advertised in its window the presence of lawyers in the building. What other choice did he have? So he walked to Court Street, glanced over the brief descriptions in the placards decorating the window, and climbed the stairs. He entered the first door whose placard said "attorney." An empty waiting room, no secretary. Just a man in a white shirt and loose tie he could see typing something through a half-open door. Hunt and peck. Hunt and peck.

Should he take a seat? He stood, uncertain, in the middle of the room. Maybe he should choose another office? But at that moment the man he'd spotted seemed to have finished his typing and called out, over his shoulder, "May I help you?"

Robert entered the small office, where there were only three chairs across from the man's desk. He remained standing until the man looked up from his machine.

The fellow was middle-aged, medium height, medium build, "no distinguishing characteristics" as witnesses were forever saying on TV police dramas. The collar that he—or someone—had no doubt buttoned up around his tie this morning, was now undone, the inexpensive, diagonally striped blue-and-yellow tie hanging limply around his neck. He was, Robert finally noticed, quite bald except for a few strands of black hair combed sideways over an otherwise shiny pate. He noticed from a nameplate on the desk that the man's name was Mr. Lombardi.

"Sit," said the lawyer, motioning toward the nearest chair.

The moment Robert was seated he added, "What can I do for you?"

"Well," Robert began slowly, "I think I need some advice."

"Shoot. What's the problem?"

Robert explained his situation as briefly as he could, including where he'd been employed until recently. Lombardi looked down at his desk and shook his head.

"Have you been doing anything to try to make money?"

Robert explained his recent application for welfare, but added that it wouldn't show up, he'd been told, for another three weeks.

"Not found any jobs so far?"

"Well, I've worked the last two Sundays passing out leaflets. All I've been able to find up to now."

Mr. Lombardi's eyebrows shot up. "Leaflets? You been passing out leaflets?"

"Yessir. Once for a Broadway show. "A Little Night Music."

"Ah, yes. Steven Sondheim. Good show!"

"So the reviewers said. If I'd had the price of a ticket I might have gone myself. Anyway, another leaflet promised a "closing-out sale" for a furniture company in the thirties in Manhattan. Madison Avenue. Once you deduct subway fare, I didn't make much. Hey! I check the ads every day to see what's available! Those two I found through the *Village Voice*."

Lombardi shook his head again. "This fuckin' economy is going to the dogs," he offered finally. "A college professor passing out leaflets. What's next?"

"I'm not the only one, you know? I met another fellow, leafing alongside me, who has a PhD in Economics. Mine is in History."

The lawyer looked down at his desk a moment, or maybe at his shoes. Robert would have bet money—if he'd had any—that the shoes were not polished.

"You gotta phone number of this person who's about to bring eviction proceedings against you?"

"Uh, yeah. Sure. Know it by heart."

Lombardi silently signaled with his hand that he should give him the number.

Robert wrote it down with his own pen but on a pad he took from the lawyer's desk. He handed it to him, and the lawyer dialed immediately.

"What's this jerk's name?"

"Profaccio, Joseph."

Mr. Lombardi smiled. "My tribe," he said.

The caller had picked up and Lombardi motioned for Robert to stay quiet.

"This Joseph Profaccio? Yes? Mr. Profaccio, my name is James Lombardi. I'm an attorney and I have a client in my office who says he's only a week or two behind in his rent and already you're threatening him with eviction. Listen, Mr. Profaccio, if you haven't noticed we're in a goddamn recession here and my client, Mr. . . ." He glanced at Robert for a name. . . "Dr. Fairweather, is an upstanding citizen who's trying the best he can to make ends meet right now, having been let go without cause from the university whose apartments you manage. Now I know this man for a long time. He's an upstanding citizen who always pays his debts and who's trying his damnedest to find a responsible job. Says he's looking for work even as we speak, and he'll pay the whole amount, bring his account up to date as quick as he's able. Understand? So, I want you to back off, Mr. Profaccio. Are you hearing me? You continue to harass and threaten my client and you'll hear from my office so fast it will make your head swim. Are we clear? I don't want to hear about this again."

He hung up and turned back toward Robert. "He won't bother you again," he said. "Go find yourself a decent job."

Robert could hardly believe his ears. "Uh, what do I owe you, Mr. Lombardi?"

Lombardi smiled. Making the sign of the cross, he said with a straight face, "Go now and sin no more."

Robert narrowed his eyes, then caught the slow smile and realized the attorney was pulling his leg. He rose and murmured a heartfelt thank-you before leaving with a considerably unburdened heart. Even as he was turning toward the door, he observed that the lawyer's attention was once again directed at his typewriter.

BECOMING A SHOE DOG

IT WAS A slow day in the ladies' shoe department and the five salesmen huddled around the cash register were exchanging stories.

There was Louis LaFarge, a small, fat, balding man with a five-o-clock shadow, in dress pants and a houndstooth jacket, who looked neither dressy nor polished. But Louis was probably the best shoe salesman in the bunch. A born huckster, as he himself liked to claim. Only yesterday he'd sold thirty pairs of ladies' shoes, and he was always hoping to best his record.

Ferris Muller was another of the five, a rather short and imperially slim fellow who wore his suit comfortably. He was dark-complexioned, with small, darting green eyes, wiry and nervous looking when not selling, much younger than Louis but just behind him in the selling sweepstakes. Beaumont Jones was a third salesman, with curly, dishwater-blonde hair, five-nine or ten, dressed neatly in an un-rumpled blue suit. He'd a wide smile and twinkling blue eyes but otherwise didn't speak much. An average performer, or so it seemed at the moment, after three weeks on the job. Harold Barlow was the fourth, the oldest among them, a man in his sixties, sedate and pleasant, a good listener and a pretty good salesman.

And then, of course, there was Robert, certainly a newbie to this profession. With his tall, broad-shouldered physique and engaging, rather dignified manner—even though his attire was Barney's, not Brooks Brothers—he did look good in his dark blue pinstripe. "You dress up nice," he'd been told in the past, and he was thankful it was still true. Unfortunately, to date, Robert had averaged only two and one-half sales a day.

He'd seen the notice in the *Times* two weeks after he'd spoken to Lombardi, the lawyer. A brand-new department store, Gimbels *East*, was opening soon on Lexington Avenue at 86th Street and was interviewing salespeople for all departments. Robert had had little experience in retail, but it was a job, so he'd applied. The manager of the shoe department, Kenneth Laramie, a tall, blonde, striking young man in his late twenties, very boyish-looking but wearing a look that immediately stamped him as an "up and comer," interviewed Robert and—though he clearly was the last one hired to fill out the staff—seemed to take a liking to him. Though he'd dismissed as barely relevant Robert's experience selling tennis shoes for Herman's Sporting Goods during Christmas recess while in college over twenty years before, he'd decided, as he put it, to "take a chance."

"Good shoe salesmen do come from all over" he'd assured Robert (no doubt while seeking to assure himself as well); "so you never know. All I'll say," he added, glancing down at Robert's feet, "is show up every morning with your shoes polished. We're selling footwear, remember?" Robert blushed, but nevertheless found he'd taken an immediate liking to Ken and sincerely hoped he wouldn't let him down. He needed the money badly, of course, and the first and only check from Gimbel's so far had already enabled him to pay a good portion of his back rent. The next paycheck might square him with his landlord.

"So, professor," drawled Louis—called Louie by everyone—as they'd gathered around the cash register during a dead spell. "Your turn." Louie, whose extra pounds at times bothered him more than others, had leaned back against a kind of podium the register rested on, to try to take some weight off his feet. "You've heard from the rest of us. So what's your story? We know you used to teach, but why aren't you doing that now?" The other salesmen perked up at this; they'd all been sharing their prior experience, but Robert had been quiet until now. As an "unusually well-educated man" (Ferris Muller's remark), he was clearly an outlier and they seemed keen to learn his tale. "We know they canned your ass," continued Louie, with a smirk, "but why didn't you just find another teaching job?" Robert shrugged and sighed. "Well, it's not so different from some of the tales you guys have told," he said. "The jobs just weren't there. Too many PhDs, is my guess. It wasn't from lack of trying, I can assure you. Let me give you an illustration of just what my job market was like. The American Historical Association—not exactly a union but the major organization in my field of college teaching—realized the problem early on and tried to help everyone in the profession who was out looking for a job. So, they decided to issue, on a quarterly basis, a book containing the professional qualifications of everyone who wanted to participate—their training, their specialties, and so on. Like mine would have identified me as an Associate Professor of History with a specialty in Russia and Eastern Europe. And at the same time, they were compiling a list of all the openings in every college and university willing to share their needs.

"Well, in one of those quarterly listings, there was a small college in the Midwest somewhere—South Dakota, I think—that said they had an opening for a 'European generalist,' meaning someone who could comfortably teach the history of Europe, and who would be offered one course in his or her specialty. In my case, Russia. I applied immediately, as soon as I could get the thing in the mail. So, it seems, did a helluva lot of other people. Three months later, when the next Quarterly book came out, it included an announcement from the same college that had posted the job. "Please, please," it said, "No more applications. We are swamped. And, by the way, the position you applied for no longer exists. In fact, if you hear of any college or university out there who could use four competent historians, please let us know, because our entire history department has just been abolished."

Robert stopped and shrugged, looking around at all his fellow shoe salesmen. "That's just how tough it was. Too many well-trained teachers, all with PhDs. Too few jobs."

All the men uttered some variant of sympathetic rumbling. Louie shook his head and turned away. Harold snickered. Beaumont sighed. Ferris exhaled a loud breath and wandered off a few steps before turning back. All their stories bore a family resemblance to Robert's; they knew what hard times were.

At that point, a woman and her daughter stepped across the invisible line that defined the ladies' shoe department. (All the carpeting on that floor was the same shade of beige.) Five men immediately perked up, but Louie—assuming his role as reigning dean of salesmen—took it upon himself to whisper, "Your turn, Robert! Go get 'er."

Robert needed no urging. He'd barely taken two strides when he realized that the woman he was approaching was dramatically beautiful. And in one more stride he had identified her. Claire Bloom. A few years earlier, he'd seen her on Broadway in Hedda Gabler and had fallen in love with her instantly from the second row.

"Good afternoon. I'm Robert Fairweather. As well as a fan. How may I help you?"

She smiled and colored slightly. He could see her daughter roll her eyes and look up at the ceiling. Of course she would. About twelve, he guessed.

"I'm afraid I'm not going to give you a very great sale," she whispered. "I just need a pair of house slippers. For myself."

There happened to be a very nice pair of leather moccasins on a riser to her right and she'd already spotted them. He took two strides, swept them off and offered them for her inspection. They were painted with red and gold flowers with green leaves.

"How about these?" he asked. She smiled, turning them this way and that, though he had the feeling she'd already made up her mind.

"They're lovely," she said. "I'll take them." She told him her size.

"I'll be right back."

There were only a few pairs of slippers in their inventory, and he knew exactly where to find them. Within minutes he'd returned with the shoes, in their box. He accepted her credit card, rang up the sale and handed her the receipt, which she tucked into her purse, offloading the package to her daughter. She smiled at Robert, and he smiled back.

"It's been lovely to meet you," he said.

"And you as well," she said. "Mr . . . Fairweather, is it?"

"It is."

"Goodbye then, Mr. Fairweather. Come along, Anna."

Robert followed them with his eyes all the way to the escalator. If he never made another sale, taking this job had been worth it.

Unfortunately, Robert's performance as a salesman continued to show little promise, so beyond the weekly draw, he was scoring few of the percentages earned for each sale. When Ken was on the floor, supervising, one day, he called Robert aside. "Listen, Kid, look at Louie."

Robert swung his head around to find Louie, who was repositioning a pair of black pumps on one of the risers.

"No, no, I mean observe him carefully the next time he conducts a sale. See how he goes about it." Robert did so at the next opportunity, while Ken was still on hand. But wasn't sure what he was seeing that was different.

When he told Ken this, Ken replied, "Okay, then let me watch you. You take the next lady that walks in, okay?"

Robert did so and did his best. After he'd slipped the requested shoe onto her foot and she'd turned it this way and that, he told her, "Say, that really looks great on you! Congrats! That looks like an excellent choice."

The woman shrugged and tried a couple of other pairs, in different colors. Ultimately, she sighed and said, "Another day, perhaps." When she'd left the area, Ken approached Robert.

"Okay, let me tell you what you're doing wrong. A woman needs to believe that the choice of which shoe she buys is hers alone. These are expensive shoes, so she's got to become convinced it's a good bargain for her. I understand what you were trying to do when you were praising how it looked, but . . . and maybe this comes from experience . . . you have to know when to back off. After a certain point they don't want to feel any more pressure. You get it? You're the provider. The facilitator. Not the salesman. Even though, of course, you are. Get it?"

Robert frowned. "Hmm. I guess so."

"Bobby, trust me when I say that an experienced shoe salesman can almost always tell, from the moment a woman walks in, whether she's going to buy anything or not. As a manager, I don't necessarily recommend acting on that but, well, it's true. You get a sixth sense. And that comes from experience."

To Robert's silence, Ken said, "Try it. Practice. You'll get the hang of it."

And he did try. He went home that very night and, after a cold dinner, consulted a brochure Ken had given him. It identified all the different parts of a lady's shoe, plus naming most of the available styles. He studied it, memorizing all the terms he could. He imagined himself back in Butler Library, cramming for his orals. He recalled storing in his brain every single ruler of the earliest Russian state, from the 8th to the 17th century, including through the period of Mongolian hegemony, including, as well, the power shift from Kievan Rus' to Muscovy. But that, of course, was a subject he'd been keenly interested in; there was no way he could become that wired when it came to women's shoes.

Did he try too hard? Who could say?

It wasn't that he sold no shoes at all, but even though he now knew what a "last" was, and the difference between a "high vamp" and a "low vamp," a "waive pump" and a "stiletto heel," what a "toe box" and a "block heel" were—all of that—he continued to have trouble finding the magic moment to back off and "let the decision be hers."

At one point Ken decided to transfer Robert to another shoe department two floors above, which was intended for a younger crowd—the platforms, the kinky shoes, the party colors, the odd shapes, the ribbons and ruffles of all types. But there were fewer customers to begin with and he had no more success there than he'd had with the older women. It began to come home to him that "selling" just might not be his game. Finally, after a substantial trial run—six months, as a matter of fact—Robert was told that he just wasn't cutting it, and they had to let him go.

Robert took away very little from his "shoe dog" experience. Little that was usable. He'd enjoyed meeting all the different guys who'd shared parts of their lives with him at Gimbels *East* but at the same time he doubted those friendships would endure. The serendipitous five minutes when he'd crossed paths with Claire Bloom were his one fond takeaway from six months as a shoe dog. *That* he would never forget.

OH, TAXI!

THE SECOND NON-ACADEMIC job that Robert Fairweather tried after losing his position at Brooklyn Quintessential University was driving a cab. After all, he loved driving, and had had a lot of experience. He'd been driving in California from whence he'd come since he was twelve; had explored the streets of Los Angeles for six years in two successive beat-up jalopies (a '39 Chrysler and a '48 Dodge) while attending school at USC and UCLA. In fact, he'd even taught driving as a part-time job while attending USC on scholarship. And as far as knowing the streets of New York City, he'd been living here for what? Five or six years now? He'd once lived in the Bronx, now lived in Brooklyn, and most of the things he'd spent any time doing outside of his classroom duties was in Manhattan, right? Surely, he knew enough about city streets by now to acquit himself as well as the next guy?

Once he'd made his application and shown up for training, though, he wasn't so sure. He'd discovered—then wondered why it should be a surprise—that he didn't know Queens or Staten Island at all. Of course, he wasn't looking to hustle fares on Staten Island, was he? But one of the things they drummed into you at the Taxi & Limousine Commission's three-day orientation was that you were *required* to take your passenger wherever he or she wished to go, at least within the five boroughs. It wasn't optional. And this was whether *the passengers* knew how to get there or not. To be sure, he'd heard rebellious murmurs from other recruits while on breaks from the classroom ("Fat Chance!" and "Not on your life, buddy!"), but he supposed that—law-abiding citizen that he'd always been—he'd best do as the authorities required. If someone wanted to go to Staten Island, he'd take them to Staten Island. After all, who would possibly want to go there if they didn't know how to get home? And what other reason could there be to go there during the four-to-midnight shift he intended to run?

So, a few misgivings and early butterflies aside, Robert started his taxi-driving career with a good bit of optimism. The first day out, however, after a few pickups and drop-offs that he thought of as purely local (no more than twenty blocks in either direction, and all in the easy-to-negotiate streets of Manhattan), scoring a total approaching $10.00 in tips, he picked up a fare around 11:00 PM in the Times Square area that was to prove considerably less soul-satisfying.

The fare in question was an older black gentleman who hailed him outside a 7ᵗʰ Avenue movie theatre. When the man poured himself into the cab, however, Robert experienced immediate misgivings. The man—in his seventies—was clearly drunk.

"Sir, do you know where it is you're headed?" he asked.

"Broog-lyn," said the passenger. It sounded as if he were speaking into a tunnel.

"Yessir. But do you have an address for me?"

"Five a-tey-for Luggan Streedt."

"Okay, let me get that down on my sheet here. 584 Luggan Street, you said?"

"LOGAN! LOGAN! FIVE ATEY-FOR L'gn Streedt."

"584 Logan Street. Got it. Uh, do you know how to get there?" (He was beginning to regret this already, but then he'd been drunk himself on occasion and always remembered how to get home, right?)

Robert heard a horn blast and looked out the rear-view window. A pair of headlights hugging his tail appeared to be getting antsy. Which was when he realized he was seeing them through drizzle. It was beginning to rain? Oh, fine! Question: Were those same protesting headlights on a cab? Maybe he could just turn over his fare to that guy? Hey, fellow! May I pass along my customer to you?

"It's my HOME!" said his passenger, defiantly. "'Course I know. Whaddya 'sink?"

"Yessir! Of course, sir. What part of Brooklyn is that?"

"O-Shun Hill."

"Ah!" Robert's heart sank. Not one of the nicer neighborhoods, or so he'd heard. But this was 1972. Last word he'd had about Ocean Hill/Brownsville was back in, what was it? 1968? Could be fine Edwardian homes by now, for all he knew. Palatial estates of the rich and famous. "Sorry, sir. Any preference for how I get to Brooklyn? Brooklyn Bridge or Manhattan? Atlantic Avenue or Flatbush?"

"Ad-Lantik Abenoo."

"Got it. Atlantic Avenue it is then."

And just as the driver behind him was leaning on his horn with greater resolve, Robert put his cab in gear and pulled out into the rain-wet street.

Okay, at least he was already facing downtown. That's a plus, right? He'd mosey over to Ninth Avenue in a block or two and head south all the way down to . . . what? It turned into . . . something. He tried to remember . . . Hudson, was it? Then, at whatever point suggested itself he'd cut over to Broadway, turn right and slither right onto the Brooklyn Bridge, which emptied on the other side into . . . Let's see, Tillary, was it? Oh no! Tillary was the cross street! He should know that. It was a stone's throw from his old university, and from the University Apartments where he lived, right? Oh, well, he knew the street in question was big, wide and you could follow it until you hit Atlantic and turn left. Right? I mean, correct. *Take Ad-Lantik*, the man had said. No problem! Piece of cake!

It was not, however, to be the sugary confection he'd supposed. The damn rain was making it difficult to see. The wipers immediately in front of him did okay, but the wiper on the non-driver's side while making a slurping racket was also failing to swipe the droplets off quite as smoothly as one might have hoped for. And of course, he needed to see out the driver's side window as well, didn't he, if he was to read the street signs? Should he roll down the window now and get a snoot-full of rain?

He glanced in the rear-view mirror. His passenger appeared to have tucked himself neatly into a corner. And fallen asleep.

In the solitude of his cab, unresponsive customer in tow, he managed to make only a few wrong turns down-town, before eventually finding his way onto Broadway as planned. He happily crossed the Bridge and found Atlantic Avenue without difficulty. So far so good! At last, he felt he was on his way.

He glanced at his meter. A whopping $11.45. The rain continued to pepper down. Soon he would have to wake his passenger in order to find out how to get to . . . Logan, was it? He glanced at the destination sheet. Yep. 584 Logan St.

He continued on a good while, passenger snoring gently in the back seat, until—craning his neck and straining his eyes to peer through the still accumulating raindrops— he passed Carlton Avenue, then Vanderbilt Avenue, and finally decided he might need to consult his fare before venturing much further. When a couple of loud invitations to "wake up" failed to rouse the man in the back seat, he concluded he'd need to stop and make sure his route was sound. Fortunately, traffic had thinned during this stretch.

At the corner of Atlantic and Washington Avenues he found a convenient place to pull over.

"Sir!" he shouted. "You're going to have to wake up. Sorry. But I need to get directions from you now." The man stirred and looked around. "Are you awake now, sir?" he asked again. "You need to tell me how to proceed from here."

The passenger shook his head. Clearly bewildered.

"Where are we?" was his first question.

"At the corner of Atlantic Avenue and Washington Avenue, sir. In Brooklyn." He waited a moment. Then, "Sir, if you don't mind, could I have your name? So I don't keep having to call you sir?"

His first noise was a belch. Then: "Belkin. Name's Belkin. Luther." He kept cranking his head around as if he were somewhere in the middle of the Gobi Desert, hoping to spot the nearest oasis. Or perhaps a camel? His attitude did not inspire confidence in Robert.

"Mr. Belkin. I have an idea. Why don't I just turn off the meter at this point. It now says $19.35. Why don't I just turn it off now and you crawl up here in the front where it will be easier to spot whatever landmarks you need. And easier to show me where to turn."

Mr. Belkin's answer was unexpected: "NINETEEN DOLLARS!"

"Nineteen thirty-five, Mr. Belkin, to be exact. So that's all I'll charge you. Okay?"

"Land 'o Goshen! All I got's a $20 bill!" He stuffed his hand in his pocket and drew it out, waving the double sawbuck like a white handkerchief of surrender.

Robert's face fell. An image of himself as the character on the bridge in Edvard Munch's 1893 painting popped into his head.

"A twenty-dollar bill," he repeated. As promised, but with greater reluctance, he reached over and flipped off the meter.

"Well, I guess we're lucky I stopped at this point," he said weakly. "Okay. Mr. Belkin, why don't you just get out now and climb up here beside me? Mind the rain now."

After Belkin had managed to seat himself in front and closed the door, Robert realized, with a shudder, he'd just made a huge mistake. ENORMOUS. GARGANTUAN. He'd been warned by the dispatcher—a Mr. Hendsch—in the roomy but oil-scented garage of the Herman Melville Taxi Company at 43rd and Tenth Avenue, that he *must not,* under any circumstances, allow anyone to ride in the passenger seat. Why? "We do this," Mr. Hendsch had announced in a voice so pleased it suggested he'd just found a way to balance the federal budget, "to assure that no one uses the cab to take his best friend or his best girl for a joyride, you understand? So, we've installed a button below the passenger seat that automatically switches on the meter whenever anybody sits there. No way can you turn it off."

Robert stared, aghast, at his meter. Sure enough: a zero, a period and two more zeros but, clearly, it was all lit up. He began to wish he could switch roles with his passenger.

"Well," he said, after a brief minute. "Don't worry about it. My fault. Just tell me where we need to go now. Continue on down Atlantic?"

Belkin looked around. "Sure. Sure, absolutely. Straight down Atlantic far as Pennsylvania Avenue. Not more'n a mile or so. Well . . . maybe two. Then we'll turn right on Pennsyl . . ." He hiccupped. ". . . vania and, let's see, a block down thataway we come to Liberty Avenue." He made elaborate shifts with his body each time he mentioned a different direction. "Then we turn left and go on Liberty a ways—lessee—about, oh, I don't know—ten blocks or so. Then—just before Fountain Avenue—we come to Logan. And there you are! Tha'ss my street! Only four blocks more to the right—maybe four and a half—and we're in front of my apartment! Easy-Peasy."

Robert wished he could share Mr. Belkin's joy, but actually, he was recalling an experience he'd had a year earlier when he was teaching a class in 17th Century English History, a country and a period he knew considerably less about than his specialty, Russia, and was therefore reliant on a detailed set of notes he'd sketched out for this particular lecture.

Suddenly he'd felt himself transported into the air above the lectern, looking down on the thirty or forty students in the lecture hall from near the ceiling. Just hovering. Yet there was that Other Him still down below, behind the podium, talking on, talking on. How, he'd wondered then, could he be in two places at once? Lecturing in complete sentences, it would appear, not missing a beat. Split into two selves he was, the one above monitoring the one below. That's how he felt now. Of course. Easy-Peasy.

He put the car into gear and eased forward. At least the rain had stopped.

A good half hour later, when they finally drew up outside of Mr. Belkin's apartment, Robert cheerfully took Mr. Belkin's twenty-dollar bill (including his sixty-five-cent tip) wished him a safe journey and began the long drive back to the cab company's garage. He would only lose his way twice on the drive back. Forty minutes after his shift was supposed to end, he arrived and pulled into the garage.

All the way back he'd been trying to calculate how much he would owe the company for this evening's adventure. Until he realized his calculations were incomplete. Wouldn't they also fine him for bringing the cab in late, cutting into the shift of the next driver?

Costly though it had been, that experience did not entirely sour Robert on his new career. It took another experience, a week later, to deal that final blow.

He'd driven carefully after his first night and had managed to accumulate a total $40 in tips so far. Not even close to what the big guys were earning but given how much he'd had to fork over after his maiden voyage, it struck him as putting a much better face on it. At least he was now out of the hole he'd fallen into that first evening.

Robert did begin to realize that the extra care he'd been taking in his driving made him lose out on a certain number of fares. He'd spot someone who seemed to be signaling for a cab, but just before he got there, another taxi would dart in front of him from another lane and, with a squeal of brakes, arrive first on the scene. What the fuck did they have? he'd growl to himself. X-Ray vision? Some sort of radar? Each of these experiences would, of course, cause Robert a bristling momentary anguish, but afterwards he would dismiss it, saying, "At least I'm not involved in a costly accident!" It took only a few days of these accumulating losses to convert him into a considerably more aggressive driver. He almost wished he could claim that now he was blowing his horn, careening into other lanes, and jamming on his brakes with the best of them, but truth to tell, years of being both a careful and a courteous driver had ruined his chances of moving into the big leagues of daredevilry.

But though it that may have largely contributed, ultimately it wasn't what stopped him. The coup de grace came, unexpectedly, on a trip to Harlem. Robert had no particular qualms about going there. Especially since he'd shifted to driving during daylight hours. But recent news reports had loudspeakered statistics about dramatic jumps in street crimes of all stripes. There'd apparently been more homicides in the first six months of 1972 than at any previous year in the city's history. And taxi drivers were reported to be among the chief targets of this mayhem.

Nor was it anything that happened with the passenger he ferried to 143rd and Adam Clayton Powell Boulevard that day that served to discourage him. The danger arrived a few seconds later. The moment his young male passenger had exited the cab and Robert had doled out his change, he spotted two figures approaching simultaneously from both the right (off the curb) and the left (from somewhere in the middle of the street). A sense of foreboding kicked in.

Among the things they'd warned you against in training was never to keep bills in your upper left hand shirt pocket, no matter how convenient it was for making change, since there'd been a recent rash of robberies based on grabbing the shirt pocket itself and ripping it off together with the money. As long as the window was rolled down, of course, which was the case on the day in question. Robert had been driving with his window open all morning, enjoying the sunshine. But thank God for that warning in the class!

Sensing what was about to happen as the two men converged—the one on the right the decoy, seeking to fix the driver's attention—Robert quickly slapped his right hand over his pocket just as the burly fellow on the left reached through the open window—and floored the accelerator. By a split second, Robert's hand arrived first, the robber's covering his and trying to pry it loose. The aggressor removed his hand only after loping alongside a few steps as the cab picked up speed, realizing he'd been foiled in his "snatch and grab."

Robert laughed as he left, feeling charged for a few moments, feeling pleased, mumbling something like, "Take that, Motherfucker!" But the damage to his psyche was there, nonetheless. This, he decided, was a bridge too far. He'd been driving a taxi for two weeks and had barely accumulated any money. And now this close call! And it could have been a lot worse. According to the news last evening, there'd been a recent rash of such incidents, several of them involving shootings. Was it worth it? This method of generating income—for him at least—didn't seem marked out for great success. Admit it, he admonished himself: you are not a cabbie.

From Harlem he drove all the way back to 10th Avenue and 43rd street, swung the car into the garage and asked for his wages. He'd need to find a better way to pay the rent.

NOW IS THE TIME

FOR ALL GOOD MEN . . . . The time is the 1970s and the place is the Upper West Side in Manhattan. Two friends, one black, one white, are talking within a modest but beautifully appointed apartment, whose dominant color is red. The bedspread is red, the rug is a deeper red. The drapes on the long windows (the ceiling is quite high) are a deep wine or maroon of a tint which complements and soothes rather than jangles against its brethren. It is in fact a symphony in red. There are scattered throw pillows on the bed which are either red or have red in them, and each seems carefully chosen to enhance the overall effect. It is as if you have entered a seraglio, but a tasteful one. Mortimer Adams, a perennial graduate student and part-time college professor who was born in Ethiopia, has a real sense of design, and his long bachelorhood has created in him a fastidious housekeeper. At the moment, he is seated on the piano bench (red threads among the deep blue covering), his back to the piano. The room is not large, but it must have a piano; you know somehow it would not be complete without a piano. And Mortimer plays that piano, seldom fiery versions of Rachmaninoff or delicate iterations of Mozart etudes, but very creditable renditions of popular melodies, including a few he composed himself. He is not a large man—five nine or five ten and slender, with deep mahogany coloring—but he has a regal bearing, and usually credits his posture to early service in the Ethiopian Royal Guards.

Despite the powerful colors, it is a quiet and peaceful room. What is neither quiet nor peaceful at the moment is Mortimer.

"But what will you *do*, my friend? You must be practical! You must make a living!" His eyes dance as he speaks; his baritone voice rises and falls in dramatic inflections. He sets down the glass of gin-over-ice on a conveniently placed red plastic-and-cork coaster, so that his arms will be free for gesturing, and almost bounces up and down on the piano bench.

His friend Robert Fairweather—a large, square-shouldered man who has recently surrendered the bushy, blonde beard trending to ginger at the edges that he wore as an academic— is depressed. He has come to Mortimer's apartment to read him a section of a novel he is in the early stages of writing. Very early. He has come all the way from Brooklyn, where he keeps an apartment in a high-rise University-owned building behind a minor center of academic learning. It is a university at which he formerly taught. Now, most days, he sits at his kitchen table with an electric Underwood portable, and tries to write.

His apartment in Brooklyn is larger than Mortimer's but has none of the panache of his friend's living quarters. Aesthetically, even spiritually, it seems much farther away than a forty-minute subway ride. There are books by the hundreds on its walls, but the walls are the bland colors selected by the management of the building. Could he not paint the walls a different color? Probably. But that is not his thing. Right now, he is rather puzzled by what his thing is.

In Robert's apartment there are no drapes on the windows, which look out on a parking lot and look down twelve floors to a neighborhood (behind the university) that is not one of Brooklyn's glitzier neighborhoods. In fact, just the opposite.

There is a mottled grey daybed in the living room and a nondescript coffee table and an orange bean-bag chair which was not chosen because its color had any relation to the hues around it. The bedroom is not large but certainly serviceable, containing a dresser that dates back to an excursion to a neighborhood thrift store. There is an adequate closet, and the room houses a double bed which sags just a bit when Robert's six-foot frame is displayed thereon.

Is it any wonder that he cherishes those occasions when he can flee from his drab and unlived-in living quarters to Mortimer's more welcoming environment?

"Practical, you say," mutters Robert. "I must be *practical*. Of course I must! You're right! This so-called novel is taking far too long and I'm running out of bread. I don't know what possessed me, except that writing is what I really feel like doing now. I paid last month's rent, but I've clearly got to find another gig."

Robert rises from the comfortable overstuffed chair that he was sprawled on and quickly sits again, takes a swig of the same beverage Mortimer is partaking of. It's all Mortimer's booze; that's how broke Robert is.

"Thanks for the hooch, by the way," says Robert. "I'll pay you back when my ship comes in."

"And your ship will come in, again, my boy, any day now. Never fear. A schooner it will be, and a handsome one. Don't worry! And you've carried me plenty of times when I was at my lowest ebb. But you must be practical, old sod. So, what will you do? MAKE A PLAN!"

"Well . . . ." The thought drifts off into a corner someplace. Robert takes another swig and drains his glass. "Okay. There's a place on Court Street in Brooklyn that's a temp agency. Miss Susan's Spectacular Temps, it's called." He makes a wry face and shrugs his shoulders. "They send you out on jobs after calling you at an ungodly hour in the morning. Mostly typing jobs, of course. Which is fine. I type fast and I don't make a lot of mistakes."

"Yes, of course! You typed your own dissertation, did you not?"

"I did. Two bloody fucking volumes!"

"Hey! Then I have an idea, my boy!" Mortimer is only three years older than Robert, but with his friend he sometimes postures as a priest or a Father-confessor.

"You should type other people's dissertations! Or Master's Theses. Or detailed, comprehensive manuscripts. After all, you know how! You know the drill! There must be a demand for people who know all those *ibids* and *op cits* and *loc shits* and stuff you're supposed to drop in as footnotes, right? You and I both live near universities. You can put notices up on your bulletin boards and I can distribute them easily here. You'll be deluged with opportunities!"

"I don't know about that. But what I do know is I need a better typewriter. So first I'll have to earn enough to buy a big, professional machine if I'm going to do that."

"You see? We've figured it out! Now, relax, you big ugly bear, and let me pour you a drink. A last drink, I might add. Then I'll loan you subway fare back to Brooklyn and send you on your way."

The very next day, a Friday, Robert put his plan into action. He went in person to Miss Susan's Spectacular Temps and signed up. The office was run by two women, who were nothing if not pleasant and accommodating. They asked him to take a typing test, which he passed with flying colors. They wanted to know if they could call him for jobs on the weekend. Are Saturdays okay? How about Sunday?

He assented to both. They assured him they'd have no problem finding him jobs. Neither of the ladies was named Susan, but he decided to squelch his curiosity and not ask about the agency's namesake.

The phone woke him up that very Sunday. They told him they had a job if he was willing to take it. Somewhere on lower Broadway. He rubbed the sleep out of his eyes, drew on pants and a tee shirt as fast as he was able, and hightailed it to the address he was given. A twenty-minute subway ride.

The firm turned out to be an insurance company, whose offices were on the 11th & 12th floor of a twelve-story building at 149 Broadway in lower Manhattan. Robert entered and took the elevator to the 12th floor, as the glassed-in directory on the main floor indicated. There was no secretary or receptionist on the other side of the heavy glass doors he pushed through, doors with writing in gold paint that identified the business as Krandall & Krandall Insurance. A man with thinning hair and a small paunch emerged from an office in front of him almost immediately, however, clutching a manilla folder. Robert introduced himself.

"Fine," he said. "I'm Cecil. Good to meet you. Follow me, please."

Robert was led down a broad stairway to the next floor and into a large conference room. Empty except for a scattering of comfortable-looking chairs and the largest rolodex Robert had ever seen, resting on the near end of a very long table. He cast his eyes about for a typewriter. There was none.

"We're updating our files," the man said.

"I thought this was a typing job."

"Oh, no. Didn't they tell you? No, actually, this job is much less demanding. More like filing. You see this rolodex? In this folder . . . ." He extracted a sheaf of typewritten pages with three columns of names on each page. "So, what I'll need you to do is to find each of the names on this list in the rolodex, extract the card and toss it. And, of course, put a check in front of each name you've done so we'll know it's been removed."

"Oh. Okay. I see. And where do I discard them?"

Cecil looked around, spotted a wastebasket and drew it over close to the chair in front of the rolodex. "Just drop them in here," he said. "That should do it. I'll be down to check on your progress in an hour or so. Okay?"

"Great! Seems simple enough. See you later."

After the man left, Robert took a moment to cast his eyes around. It was a lovely conference room, but there were no lights on. The drapes on the long windows had been pulled aside, however, so light from the outside flooded the room. Without the overhead lights blazing, however, the effect remained gloomy. Several large oil portraits on the walls, all unlit. A deserted castle, perhaps. Or a mausoleum?

"Just my peculiar imagination," he whispered to himself. "Okay, Fairweather. Let's get to work."

He sat down in the swivel chair, whirled himself around once, just for the fun of it, and pulled the rolodex closer. It was, of course, in alphabetical order. The whole point of a rolodex. The names on the typed pages were not, but that didn't matter; all you had to do was spin the giant rolodex to the proper place in the alphabet and search for the name. Piece of cake.

He'd done about ten names when he stopped. It suddenly hit him. One of the cards in the rolodex had scrawled across the bottom of it, in blue ink, the word "deceased." And what he must have unconsciously realized earlier suddenly struck him with the force of a revelation. This was an insurance company. The names he was removing from the rolodex, and tossing cavalierly into the wastebasket, were men (and some women) who were all dead. He was effectively tossing dead bodies into the trash.

He stopped a moment. "Shit," he said to himself. "This is kind of morbid. I mean, I understand. They need to update their files. But still." He suddenly felt, had he been a Catholic, he ought to be crossing himself each time he tossed someone into the bin. He shook his head and sighed. "Kind of grim," he said. "And I'm doing it so wantonly. Shouldn't I say, 'Hail Mary?' Or 'Godspeed?' Or something like that? Each time I acknowledge that these guys have kicked the bucket?"

He thought a moment. He felt like a funeral director. Thereafter, he said "Rest in peace, Mr. Thackeray. Rest in peace, Mr. Clausewitz. Rest in peace, Mrs. Goforth . . . ." But that lasted only another ten minutes before he gave it up and said to himself, "C'mon, Fairweather. Don't be daft. You're not a funeral director. You're a cleaner. You're the guy who comes in after a murder—or a slaughter—has been committed and wipes up the blood and the guts and makes sure that the house or the bar or the place of business looks as spic and span as it did before. That's your job."

And he continued for the rest of the day with little comment, dropping dead bodies into their final coffins.

His second assignment, the very next day, was also in the Wall Street environs, but he wasn't expected to be there until ten o'clock. Since this was a proper workday and he had time to dress, he decided to don a suit and tie for the occasion. And he carried his briefcase, with a notebook and several pencils inside, should there be an opportunity during his lunch hour to scribble poems or suggest scenes from the novel he hoped to have time to work on during his lunch hour. At least he hoped there'd be a lunch hour.

The subway proved timely, with no interruptions, so he arrived early, at 9:45, found the right floor, and was greeted by a tall, friendly-looking fellow who emerged from an interior office.

"Hi," said Robert, extending his hand. "My name is

Robert Fairweather and I'm from Miss Susan's Spectacular Temps."

"Oh, hi," said the man. "Good to meet you. Richard Condon here. Uh, why don't you have a seat out here somewhere while we wait?" He indicated the exterior area where there were a number of desks, all equipped with impressive-looking typewriters—for secretaries, Robert assumed—and, with a pleasant smile, disappeared back into his private office, though he left the door ajar. Five minutes later he reemerged, looking a bit nonplussed, and offered, "Oh, say, while you're waiting, can I get you a cup of coffee or anything? Our man who called your company in the first place, the one who has the extra workload, hasn't come in yet, but . . ."

Robert was surprised—shocked might be a more accurate description—but tried not to show it. "That would be great!" he said, smiling. "Black please, if that's okay. No milk or sugar." He'd stood up when the man emerged from his office, but now reseated himself in the same chair.

In a matter of minutes, the smiling man—Mr. Condon, he remembered— returned with his coffee. Robert rose to receive it, then retreated to his chair, whispering his thanks. He wondered what on earth his task for today was going to be? But he also wondered—this was truly puzzling—whether all this company's secretaries and typists got this kind of royal treatment? This was a company of brokers, he understood, not an insurance firm like yesterday's, and he had absolutely no idea what he ought to expect. And where was everybody? It was now considerably past ten o'clock.

Several minutes later—Robert had drunk most of his watery coffee and could feel himself already on the verge of needing a bathroom break. He still endeavored to look as pleasant and expectant as possible. At that moment his greeter emerged once more from his office and strolled over to where Robert sat. Robert offloaded his coffee to the nearest desk and rose again.

"So, you're from the temp agency?" the broker said, smiling and rocking back and forth a bit, looking for all the world like he was in a mood to chat.

"Yes," said Robert. "Miss Susan's Spectacular Temps, we're called."

"Right, right! Miss Susan's . . . right . . .well, it's awfully nice of you to show up. And so early! We actually have one of your people coming over here this morning." He checked his watch. "In fact, should be here by now."

Suddenly, Robert understood. *One of your people?*

"Uh, I think there's been a misunderstanding, Mr. Condon. Actually, I am that person. I'm your typist. The agency sent me over here on a typing assignment."

Mr. Condon looked flustered but eventually nodded and chuckled. Robert wanted to say—longed to say, in his most professional voice—"Hey, don't worry about it, I get that all the time," but managed to hold his tongue.

The man with the pieces to be typed eventually showed

up and Robert worked until six o'clock that evening, cleaning up all the backload that the gentleman asked him to do. He managed to keep the smirk off his face until he got into the elevator going home.

After a few weeks (he didn't bother to count how many) of fairly steady jobs at this or that place of business on Wall Street or in midtown, Robert had set aside what he thought was a satisfactory amount to engage the next phase of his work plan. He'd heard about a place on Fulton Street, downtown Manhattan, that was a typewriter haven for new and reconditioned machines.

He visited the store on a Saturday. The owner was genial looking, a tall, bulky man with short white hair through which one could not help noticing a glistening pink skull. He wore a full-length leather apron and Robert luxuriated in all the beautiful new and used machines scattered roundabout, both portable and office: Remingtons, Underwoods, IBMs, Olympias, Brothers, Royals, Smith-Coronas, Olivettis, and seemingly countless others, both electric and manual. The shop smelled deeply of ink and work, and Robert reveled in it. It called to mind his high school days when, as an aspiring journalist, he would visit places where newspapers were printed, where he learned to read type upside down as it was fitted into a "bed" by a Lino-typist.

"I need to buy a good typewriter," he began, after the

only other customer left the store and he could at last catch the eye of the proprietor. "I have an Underwood portable, but I'm going to be typing professionally—dissertations and such—and I need a sturdy, dependable workhorse of a machine."

The man smiled and cast his arm in a long circuitous arc around his shop. As you can see," he said, "that's what we do. New or used?"

"Well, I guess . . . uh . . . used, but reconditioned."

"Of course, reconditioned! I'm Charles Womack and that's what I do. I consider it my art. A reconditioned typewriter is as good as a new one."

"Well, I'm operating on a tight budget right now, but I've managed to save $60. What can I buy with that?"

The man sighed and looked away a moment. "Very little, I'm afraid. That's really low-balling it, young man. Cheapest office typewriter I could sell you is priced at $120."

Robert's face fell. "Shit," he muttered softly. "I guess I had no idea."

After a beat or two, arms folded across his chest, the man offered, "May I make a suggestion? Why don't you consider renting? On a monthly basis? I'm afraid the cheapest I could do that would be $65 a month."

Robert had never considered that option.

"If you choose to do that," Mr. Womack continued, "I could outfit you with a very nice Remington machine, completely reconditioned. And I'd deliver it to your home or office, wherever you like, at no additional charge. You wouldn't even have to give me the whole amount up front. Twenty bucks and you can take it away, make your money and pay me at the end of the month. A few months down the road or a year, whenever you're done, I'll take it back, no questions asked. Or if you're able to buy it at that time, no sweat. We can do that too."

He paused a moment, then added, "Anything goes wrong, of course, I would replace and repair immediately. But it won't. Not with that machine."

Since Robert didn't see his way clear to another alternative, he took Mr. Womack up on his offer. The typewriter was delivered on Saturday in the afternoon, after he'd spent the earlier part of the day putting up notices on the various bulletin boards around Brooklyn Quintessential University. Saturday evening, he delivered a batch of notices to Mortimer, who dutifully spread them around Columbia. By Tuesday he'd already had a phone call from a graduate student who needed her dissertation typed. Psychology. She was local—from BQU—and he invited her over immediately.

Diana Haversham was tall and rangy, with a long, rather equine face. Not very talkative, but pleasant enough. She was dressed in thrift shop attire, which made him think: "Ah! One of us!" By that weekend she'd delivered the bulk of her material. Unfortunately, the remaining pages of her thesis were destined to dribble in as a diminishing series of afterthoughts and addenda. Which parts went where was often a question better left to soothsayers or those trying to divine water with a forked stick.

So, in order to stay afloat—to stay un-hungry and hydrated as well as to have a couple of quarters left over for his laundry—Robert began to accept scattered assignments from Miss Susan's during the day, and pecked away at Miss Haversham's dissertation evenings and weekends. From him, she would collect the pages on an appointed evening and return a few days later with any necessary corrections. And there *were* corrections—both from things he'd mistyped and hadn't caught (her handwriting sometimes made him gnash his teeth), as well as the little surprises when her dissertation advisors had asked her to *pleeeeeeze* change a word or two, which more often than not meant re-typing a whole page.

Nevertheless: Page by page, bottle by spent bottle of whiteout, the task was at last finished. Not a perfect job, in his view, and a good deal slower than he'd imagined, but it got done. The psychologist-to-be had proved a very average writer, and he'd frequently have to steel himself against the urge to improve her prose. Just get the job done, he'd tell himself crossly each time the impulse visited; you're not getting paid to help this lassie win a Nobel Prize.

After almost two months of this, Robert felt as if he'd dug a gopher hole and pulled the dirt in after him. Not only had he made less money than he'd hoped from Miss Pettigrew (as he'd come to call her), but not another soul had rung his phone to offer him a fresh project. Most damaging of all, to both his psyche and his pocketbook, his typing—and its all too necessary corrections—had proved several light years slower than he'd expected. Throwing up his hands, he called Womack to reclaim his typewriter and went crawling back to Miss Susan's with his tail between his legs, begging for every assignment they could throw his way. Not only had he lost countless hours of sleep with this project and worked himself to a frazzle; he'd barely cleared thirty bucks' profit from the whole ordeal.

Three months down the road from his abandoned dissertation-typing project, Robert felt that—although still a bit glum—he was finally getting over his embarrassment at having labeled himself, on all those notices he'd put up on bulletin boards both at BQU and Columbia, "The Scholar's Typist." What an unfortunate episode of braggadocio that had been! The first few weeks after having jettisoned that particular enterprise, when he'd get the occasional call from some graduate student enquiring about his prices, he'd be grateful no one could see his face turn crimson as he explained that he was "no longer providing that kind of service." A few times he'd even stooped to the lie that "Sorry, I'm just too busy at the moment to take on additional work," and hung up as soon as humanly possible.

He did feel himself lucky that Miss Susan's had found him, very shortly after he'd returned, a semi-permanent assignment at a paint manufacturer in Brooklyn. Called Morgan's Paints, it was located near the Smith and Ninth loop of the F train only a few stops from his apartment (though distressingly, for a paint factory, not too far from the Gowanus Canal). Robert decided it would be a case of "biting the hand that feeds" should he enquire where their chemical runoff was steered, so he held his tongue.

And it was a nice gig, actually. Pleasant and easy. Miss Susan's pay scale was a tad less than it would be for Saturday or Sunday postings on Wall Street, but the slow pace of the workload—giving him an opportunity to write poems or letters or whatever he chose to do in his spare time—more than made up for it.

What they actually wanted at Morgan's was a secretary, not just a typist. So, he would answer the phone, log in orders, call customers back to answer this question or that, type up the occasional report and, beyond that, his time was his own. Not a bustling office. The phone on his desk actually rang an average of three times a day.

Meanwhile, Robert continued to scan the want-ads in the *Times* for more suitable positions, which he brought to work in his briefcase along with his notepads and pencils. And what he was now thinking of as "suitable" was anything that might be connected to writing, which remained his dominant interest. It had recently occurred to him that what he needed to do was get into *publishing* in some capacity or another, and that could surely lead to other things? So his eyes would search eagerly through the newspaper to find anything that smacked of that.

And three months into his gig with Morgan's, he finally spotted it: a reviewing service called Feathercroft. The firm catered principally, it seemed, to libraries. They would receive galleys from publishers a few months before the books went to press and prepare reviews for the sake of the buyers at the New York Public Library—all branches—as well as other libraries, large and small, across the land. In the "want ad" he spotted, Feathercroft had given notice that it was looking for a person—male or female—to write book reviews as well as attend to "a few other" unspecified duties. When Robert saw that, he thought he might actually jump for joy. "Yes!" he told himself, in a low voice lest others hear, "That's what I'm talking about! That's my leg in the door! I'll get to show off my writing skills and from there . . . ." He glanced up and around the roomy Morgan executive office (located directly over the factory), where his desk sat next to a large picture window a good thirty yards from Mr. Jonas, the company's vice president, and was happy to note that no one seemed to have heard his muffled exclamation of joy.

Even before he'd had lunch the day of his discovery, Robert had called for an appointment, asking that it be as late in the day as possible. It was scheduled for 4:30 that afternoon, and when he asked his boss, Mr. Farnsworth, if he could leave a bit early, there were no objections. So at 3:45 he left Morgan's to mount the subway and head for the Village, which was where Feathercroft's office was located. Once arrived, he marched through a good-sized waiting area with handsome leather couches and roomy chairs, and knocked at an open door which led into a long room with multiple desks and a very busy atmosphere. Just past the entrance on the right was a small office surrounded by corrugated plastic windows. Inside he spotted a woman at a desk who'd been absorbed in a pile of manuscripts, but who looked up at the sound of his knock. She smiled broadly and—a tall woman—unfolded herself from her swivel chair and came toward him with an outstretched hand.

"Hi," she said. "I'm Margaret Atherton. And you must be Mr. Fairweather."

Although Robert was a bit nervous, her welcoming smile set his mind at rest immediately.

"Please," she said, "take this seat next to my desk and we'll get right to it." She took the curriculum vitae he offered her and began reading it the moment she sat back down.

She was a woman in her forties, he guessed. A green silk blouse and a knit skirt of a darker hue. She had a somewhat narrow nose and a generous mouth, but the overall effect was pleasing. Her light brown hair was worn short, but with wisps curling around her ears. A green comb in her hair complemented the blouse.

When she'd speed-read the resume, she placed it on top of the manuscript she'd been perusing and smiled, but her face was full of questions.

"Well," she said. "My, my, Mr. Fairweather. Right off the bat I'd say you look a touch overqualified for this job. So. What made you decide to apply?"

He looked down a moment, then returned her gaze and smiled what he hoped was his most winning smile.

"Miss Atherton," he began, "The academic profession is no longer where I choose to hang my hat. I was as surprised as anyone when I was let go from the university where I taught, only to discover that there are basically no teaching jobs anywhere. Too many PhDs for too few jobs, and too few undergraduates attracted to history these days. Especially in my area. As you may know even better than I do, jobs of a certain kind are almost impossible to find these days. Right now, Miss Atherton, I'm typing for a living."

She looked shocked, then deeply concerned.

"Yes," he said. "Working for Miss Susan's Spectacular Temps, as a typist. Because I haven't been able to find anything else at all of a professional nature. At all. Miss Atherton, I beg of you. I have—have almost always had—ambitions to be a writer. And knowing I need to get my foot in the door somehow, this job—and the opportunity to demonstrate those skills by writing book reviews—seemed like a good fit to me. I really need a suitable job and I think this one would probably please me a great deal. I'm sure I'd love it."

She looked down, shook her head sadly. "Oh, my. Mr. Fairweather, I hear what you're telling me and I sympathize. Really, I do. But you may have an exalted view of what we need here. I hope the ad was not misleading. Yes, you would be able to do reviews now and then, but we also need someone to open mail and stuff. There'd be a lot of that, mixed in with a few reviews. Would you be okay with that?"

"Absolutely. After all, that's part of what I'm doing now, only I don't get the opportunity to do book reviews. This puts me closer to the world of writing that strongly draws me."

She sighed and looked away a moment. "I don't know, Mr. Fairweather. I just don't. . ."

"Please? Could you give me a chance? A tryout, so to speak?"

After a moment of looking into the desperation in his eyes, she said, "Ok, look. Of course. Let me suggest an assignment. I'll ask you to write a couple of book reviews, shall I? You'll take the galleys and, whenever you're able to return them with your reviews attached, I'll look at them and see what I think. Ok?"

Robert's whole face lit up. "That's grand," he said. "I'd love that!"

She rose and called out to one of her employees, of

which there appeared to be exactly five, scattered in a single row along a corridor that stretched away from her cubicle. Rather like staring into a tube. Twice as many desks, though, as people.

"Amy?" she called. "Could you bring me the two most recently arrived galleys?"

When she handed them to him, he was beaming. "When do you need them by?"

"Oh, there's really no hurry, Mr. Fairweather. Or should I say, *Dr.* Fairweather? Two weeks? Three? We're not on any tight deadline with these books at the moment. Whenever you're done, bring them back to me and we'll take it from there."

Robert slipped the galleys into his briefcase and rose from his chair. He felt buoyant. He grabbed her hand and squeezed. He felt an impulse to kiss her but didn't. "Thank you! Thank you!" he said. "Thank you for the opportunity. You won't be disappointed."

On the subway home, he examined his galleys. It was the first time he'd ever handled these long, ink-speckled pages and it was somehow thrilling. These were actual books, almost ready to be published! One was a biography of a nineteenth century American labor organizer, the other a book about the intertwined careers of two early Tin Pan Alley musicians. He didn't know a great deal about either subject, but so what? Wasn't that what books were all about?

That was a Monday, and exactly one week later he was back at Miss Atherton's office. He knocked and she looked up, appearing surprised to see him again so soon. Nevertheless, she accepted his pages and asked him to take a seat in the waiting room; she'd be with him shortly. He immediately chose the soft leather couch he'd noticed earlier. Through a large picture window, he could see bodies swirling past on the bustling noon-hour sidewalk, but he was oblivious to who they were or even whether they were young or old, or women or men. Periodically (it had been mere minutes) he'd close his eyes and articulate, in a low voice, a single word: "Please."

Twenty minutes later Miss Atherton left her office, entered the waiting area, handed him back his two reviews, took the large leather armchair and looked at him with mournful eyes.

"*Dr.* Fairweather," she said. "I'm sorry. I can't hire you. You're simply overqualified. These reviews are quite wonderful. You should have my job. And trust me, I'm not moving over. I need a job too. I'm sorry, Mr. Fairweather. I truly am."

Then she rose, shook his hand and turned away. But stopped and spun back around before Robert had even taken a step.

"Believe me, Robert, I sympathize. I've been at this job only eleven months. I was a PhD student myself, in language and literature. I saw the handwriting on the wall just over a year ago and heard about this position through the graduate school grapevine when its previous editor died. These are hellish days, Robert. And I wish you all the luck in the world."

THE ART OF LETTERS

She wore green because it was the season for green. He felt lust because it was the season for lust. A green ribbon in her hair, a green sheath dress, green stockings, green shoes. There was a green plant on the table . . . .

I T WAS NEARING Christmas. Robert Fairweather read his prose poem, "Green"—about love and lust and color and continuity— in a sonorous, dramatic voice and was pleased to feel from the audience what was called in those times "good vibrations."

The place was a café on the Upper East Side called Dr. Doolittle's. It had a platform at one end of the main space and there was a bar off to the side. Readings at Doolittle's were a weekly affair, always on Sunday afternoon. They were curated by a small, strong-willed woman named Charlotte Gray, and she'd been staging them for forty years. Ms. Gray, who happened, by coincidence, to be wearing a green dress on this occasion, seemed particularly pleased.

Robert shared the platform with four readers, all

occupying folding chairs, though at this moment Robert was just retreating from the mike. He knew none of the other readers. All here by invitation. The two young fellows to his right were forgettable, at least to Robert's way of thinking, or their poetry was, but the woman to his left was not. She'd been the performer before him; Robert was the last reader.

He imagined the woman to be a bit younger than he— Robert was nearing forty—and he found her striking. She was visually dramatic: long neck, flaming red hair piled on top of her head Edwardian style, a markedly erect posture. She wore a full-skirted, pleated violet dress down to her ankles, and he imagined: perhaps petticoats underneath? A nineteenth century Gibson Girl come to life in mid-to-late twentieth century New York?

He'd given the occasional reading around the City during the days he'd been a history professor at Brooklyn Quintessential University, and keeping this pursuit afloat was one of the few things that gave him a sense of continuity, a stabilizing link during these days (weeks? months?) following what he'd come to think of as The Great Departure. Poetry readings were a link he sometimes felt an almost desperate need of. Sometimes there was even a bit of money to be had; a hat was passed at the end of each reading, and the performers split the take. In earlier, cushier times—he'd been a featured reader at one venue or another since 1969—he might have referred to this as "chump change," but in the more constrained circumstances of the Seventies, it was utterly welcome: he was happy for anything he could get.

After the applause, and the smiles, and the chit-chat, and the shaking of hands with Ms. Gray and the other performers, once the proceeds had been divided and stuffed into pockets and purse, Robert noticed that the lady to his left had thrown on her shawl (another stylistic tic of her appearance) and was leaving. He scrambled to get his papers gathered, his briefcase closed, coat and cap on and, after pushing through the swinging doors and outside into the crisp December air, he spotted her maybe a dozen yards ahead, walking briskly uptown toward the subway. He yelled a greeting.

She stopped and turned, waiting for him to catch up.

"Sorry," said Robert, when he was close enough that he didn't need to shout. "I just wanted to meet you and tell you I enjoyed your poetry."

"And I yours," she said. "Thank you. I'm C.K. C.K. O'Connor."

"Robert Fairweather." They shook hands. "I was also struck, I must say, by your appearance. You're not only lovely, but very dramatically so. Do you mind if we walk a bit together?"

She laughed. "Not at all. You're not so bad yourself."

When they'd fallen into an easier pace, Robert said,

"What do you do, then, C.K.? When you're not reading poetry at bars?"

"I'm an actress," she said. "And I sing. Light opera. The occasional church gig. And yourself?"

She allowed him to accompany her all the way to the Hotel Opera on 72nd Street and Broadway—a once fine establishment that had fallen on less prosperous times—and even invited him up to her room. She told him she'd recently separated from her husband—also an actor—and was hoping to find an apartment of her own in the near future.

They talked as they shed their outer garments, then grew quiet as they discarded everything else, never taking their eyes off each other. They made love on her narrow single bed. Though not violins and roses—at least for Robert—it was a pleasurable and deeply welcome experience, marking, as it did, the end of a long drought in his sex life. They both giggled like schoolchildren afterwards.

When, a short while later, Robert was dressing to leave, and just pulling on his boxer shorts, C.K. (he now knew her as Chloe Kayleigh O'Connor but she strongly preferred C.K.) suddenly exclaimed: "Oh, goody! Are you a righty or a lefty?"

"Beg pardon?"

"I've always wondered, and kept track of, which of my men wore their balls on the left side and which on the right."

Robert looked at her in puzzlement. "I can't say I've

ever thought about that. I've just pulled on my shorts without noticing."

"Well, where are they now?"

Robert pulled his shorts away from his body and looked down. "I suppose you would say they're . . . on the right."

"Yes! And you're right-handed, as well, correct?"

"I am, but surely that's just coincidence!"

"Oh, I don't doubt that there's a pattern. I'm making it my business to figure it out. So far, it seems to hold true." She seemed delighted, very pleased with herself.

"Well, there you are then," said Robert. "You learn something new every day. Even when you're the subject." Though what he was thinking was that he'd never felt more like an object. Still, she was a singular and intriguing woman. He shook his head and laughed.

They continued to see each other, but only occasionally. Each encounter, however friendly and pleasurable, seemed at the same time somehow staged—or formal, perhaps—as if they were participants in an ongoing experiment. He often wondered: was this science or sex? They never went out, never had dinner, went to a bar, took in a show. She was often engaged when he called asking about a particular evening, or afternoon. Which of "her men" was she entertaining then, he wondered? And was this man a "righty?" Or a "lefty?" Yet when she was not available it amused rather than distressed him since he never felt romantically involved. But even these encounters waned, then stopped.

A month or so later, on a Saturday, Robert sat inside a small coffee shop on 57th Street, squeezed into an undersized two-person booth waiting for a guest to show up. He'd already downed a cup of coffee and a second steaming cup sat in front of him, which he was trying not to drink until his guest arrived. He squirmed nervously. He was about to interview Cleveland Amory for information about an article he'd pitched to *New York Magazine*. Robert glanced at his watch. Was this guy going to show or not? It had been Amory's suggestion they meet here, near the office of the Fund for Animals, which he ran, and this had been the only booth available. He glanced at his watch. The man was already ten minutes late.

This meeting was part of a new strategy of Robert's for earning money in a way that would also satisfy what he'd now decided was his principal interest: writing. Other people were earning money by writing, were they not? Perhaps he could too? As a freelance journalist? So the first idea he'd had, — after overhearing at a party thrown by his dear friend Mortimer, that one of the revelers kept a llama in his rather spacious Upper East Side apartment —was to research and discover how many other exotic animals might be sequestered in New York City dwellings. He'd thought it might be a good human-interest story, and so he'd cold-called the editorial offices of *New York Magazine* and pitched them the idea. An editor named Nick Spulvaney had listened to him and said, "Well, I don't know you, Mr. Fairweather, never seen you in print before, but it sounds like something we might be interested in. Why don't I say we'll take it on spec?"

"And what does that mean, exactly? On spec?"

"You *are* new to this game, aren't you?" had been the editor's reply. "It means if it turns into a story that is lively and that we feel our readers would appreciate, then we'll take it, and pay you for it. But we have to see it first."

And that was that. So Robert, whose day-job since he'd been ousted from his position as Assistant Professor of Russian History at Brooklyn Quintessential University, was typing wherever he'd been assigned by Miss Susan's Spectacular Temps (when he wasn't passing out leaflets or doing inventory), had decided to try launching himself into a career as a free-lance journalist. After all, wasn't that what his earlier life had been pushing toward? Before he'd diverted into the field of Russian studies as a college sophomore, he'd been on a scholarship that expected him to become a journalist. And hadn't that been his trajectory? His sister—two years older than he—had been the editor of the country high school paper in the California farming area where he'd grown up, and when he got to high school he'd served as editor for two years himself. The paper had won awards and, at conferences, so had he, particularly for editorial writing. He'd even attended, on scholarship, between his junior and senior years, the National High School Institute for Journalism at Northwestern University.

A year later he'd enrolled at the University of Southern California after winning a journalism scholarship. In fact, he'd been told he was on track to become the editor of USC's award-winning *Daily Trojan* if he continued on that path. So here he was now, hoping against hope that it was possible to reanimate an earlier passion.

Precisely at 2:15 Mr. Amory burst through the revolving door with all the subtlety of a Sherman tank. Robert was himself a large man, six-feet tall, broad-shouldered and just south of 200 pounds. But Amory was a mountain: six-four, a face you could imagine had been cleaved from stone, a frizzy mop of black hair selectively shading to gray, and the bulk of a heavyweight wrestler. Robert held up his hand to signal him, and Amory smiled and lurched over to the booth.

"Robert Fairweather, Mr. Amory. So pleased to meet you."

"Same here, same here." He looked around the shop. "I don't think this is going to work, do you? Two big guys like us? Let's see if we can get a larger booth. Hey, Dominic!" He signaled to the owner, busy behind the counter. Dominic was at his side so quickly you'd have thought he had a scooter. "You think you can find a more accommodating booth for us two bohunks?"

"Yessir, Mr. Amory. Of course! That booth against the window is this moment now become empty. Please to follow me."

A family of four were scrambling out of the booth as he

spoke, and he quickly corralled one of his waiters to shift Robert's coffee and give "these distinguished gentlemen" menus.

As soon as they were settled, Amory turned to Robert and asked, "Okay, so what's this article you're writing, Mr. Fairweather? My secretary tells me it's something about animals in New York City?"

Robert smiled. "Indeed, sir. *New York Magazine* has taken an idea of mine on spec so I'm trying to flesh it out now. It's about all the exotic animals that seem to be kept as pets here in the City. Right now, I'm just trying to get as much information on that subject as I can."

"Hmm. You realize, I suppose, that's not something I particularly approve of, this sequestering of wildlife in apartments but you're absolutely right, it's out there. 'Course if you're a real animal lover and you've got the space and you're willing to put in the time and care for them properly, that's not so bad. In my opinion, that's not the case ninety-nine percent of the time. I take it you're asking my opinion on the matter, right? The opinion of my animal rights organization, The Fund for Animals?"

"Definitely, sir. And that will . . ."

"Eighty-six the *sir*, Mr. Fairweather. Call me Cleveland."

"Oh! Well, if you prefer, s—uh, Mr. Amory. Cleveland. Wow! I may have trouble with that. I'll think I'm referring to a city in the Midwest. Where I've never been, by the way. And have you? Been to Cleveland, that is?"

Amory smiled. "Nary once, oddly enough. Been all over the US as well as many parts of the known world, but never in Ohio."

Robert's turn to smile. "Good to know. Though I don't expect it to be part of this particular article. Anyway, as I was saying, your point of view will certainly be part of the story. But I'm after a bit more than that as well, if I may. I know about a few of these animals . . . rather by accident, I have to say . . . but I'm trying to gain a sense of the number, the whole picture. How many might there be? Of what types? And where are they? Are we talking a lot or a little? I figured that you, with your finger on the pulse of animal lovers everywhere, might be able to steer me to more information about them than I currently have. I'm just at the beginning here."

They talked for almost an hour. Two more cups of coffee and a couple of Danishes had been consumed before the interview was done. Robert acquired a lot of information and got ideas for where to dig up more. Veterinarians Amory knew who treated exotic animals in the city. The Zoos. The Health Department (even though Amory was not a fan). Those interviews, Robert was sure, would eventually lead to other sources.

With respect to numbers, Robert would eventually conclude that the total number of exotic animals sequestered in NYC apartments was likely upwards of a quarter million. Amory estimated the monkey population alone to be about 25,000, which blew Robert's mind until Sidney Weber of Bide-a-Wee Homes, said he'd place it closer to 100,000. Those numbers startled Robert. He also learned there were 4,282 animals (an exact count) in the five zoos , plus an additional 10,000 kept in various laboratories, institutes, and educational establishments. He was assured as well that the estimated quarter million exotic pets did not include dogs, cats, hamsters, gerbils, fish and birds, who were not considered "exotic" at all. And, although he was able to locate for certain only one caracal lynx, one wolf, and one llama, he finally decided he would call his article "Llama in the Living Room: New York's Underground Zoo."

But what startled Robert most that first afternoon was the direction in which Amory managed to steer the conversation in the last twenty minutes of their time together. He began by asking Robert about his roots. His birth in Oklahoma, his growing up in a sandy, dusty, country environment in California's San Joaquin Valley, the fact that he'd done a lot of low-level jobs on that corporation farm, hard jobs, long hours, short pay.

"You know what," he said finally, "I've got a suggestion for you, Robert. And I'm serious about this. You know what I'd like to see happen? One of the biggest perpetrators of animal cruelty today in this country, here in the 1970s, believe it or not, is dogfighting. Horrible business. Goes on all over the South: Georgia, Mississippi, Alabama, wherever. A lot of money to be made; a lot of wonderful animals getting destroyed. One way or another. Now, here's what I'd like to see. We need some research, some undercover stuff to dig out the real extent of it. How many dogs? How many people involved? How much money changing hands? One organization or many? I've been looking for a long while to find someone I thought would be good at infiltrating those organizations, so we could get enough information to create a public outrage about it and stomp them into oblivion. They have turned and continue to turn wonderful animals into killers, and all of those noble dogs—winners or losers—ultimately destroyed by such awful, inhumane practices. Hey, look at you, Robert! You're a big guy with a common touch. You look like someone who could take care of himself and at the same time, born in Oklahoma you're practically a Southerner yourself. You can speak the lingo, walk the walk, talk the talk . . . ."

During all this extended monologue Robert tried to keep his features level and unreadable but found it a struggle. *What?* he was saying in his mind. Was he kidding? This well-regarded man—a patrician if there ever was one—was suggesting that he'd like to recruit him, *Him!*, to go down South (Go South, young man!) and infiltrate a bunch of illegal dog-fight operations? Because he thought Oklahoma was part of the South? He wanted him to go undercover? Like the FBI? Or the CIA? Would he get a little Special Forces training to boot? *Sir!* he was screaming inside his head. Or Cleveland, as you've asked me to call you! *I am not a commando, nor ever wished to be. Until a few short years ago I was a college professor talking about abstruse matters like philosophy and history. I'm not someone who's either gifted or experienced at bare-knuckle brawling. True, I read a magazine as a young teenager that suggested if I ever confronted someone trying to choke me or batter me the best use of my time was to gouge their eyes out, and I briefly thought what a useful skill that would be, but Sir! Really! Did I tell you I used to teach Russian Intellectual History? Who in God's name do you think I am?*

And at the same time, he was thinking: *he's offering me a job here! I've been thirsting for a job for some years now and he's offering one! I have to admit that part of me feels flattered by his notion of my survival skills, my undercover potential, much as I think, at the same time, that I'd rather be anyplace else than arm-wrestling a bunch of grizzled, over-muscled, Day's Work-chewing Southern yokels into changing their minds about their misguided, cruel ways of treating animals. I imagine they'd be equally interested in handing me my ass in a sling! Thanks but no thanks!*

They ended the conversation with Robert thanking Amory for his time and all that wonderful information, and . . . as for that other matter . . . he'd give it some thought, but it didn't seem quite the way he saw his life going right at this particular moment.

Amory left the coffee shop first, and Robert waved him

on his way, saying he needed to make some notes before all these great ideas left him. But he shook his head repeatedly, as if it were stuffed with sawdust. And of course, since he was the petitioner, he picked up the tab.

"Roll out the barrel! We'll have a barrel of fun!
"Roll out the barrel! We'll get our blues on the run!"

Robert and his friend Mortimer were singing at the top of their lungs around Mort's piano, belting out a song chosen to chase away Robert's blues. When he'd arrived at Mort's Upper West Side apartment forty-five minutes earlier, to say he was glum was like describing a tidal wave as a ripple in a quiet pool.

"They didn't take it!" had been the first words out of Robert's mouth, the door barely opened. "They rejected me, Mort!! I worked my ass off for three weeks—weekends and evenings only, of course, because I needed to keep going with my day job or I wouldn't eat—and this is the result? I'll never write anything 'on spec' again! What the hell was I thinking? I can't even make it as a free-lance writer! Now what am I going to do? Type other people's prose or numbers for the rest of my life?"

Mortimer had comforted, "There, there, you big, ugly bear! Calm down. Let me pour you a dram of scotch and you can tell me all about it."

So his friend had given him a stiff tumbler of Glenfiddich and listened while Robert unrolled his tale. Later, he'd asked if Robert had brought with him the 'animal story,' as he called it. Unsurprisingly—he knew his friend—Robert had. And after he'd looked it over, he shook his head sadly and said, "Look, Robert. It starts brilliantly! That's very good writing! I don't think they rejected it because of the opening. But the ending, man! It's like you depart from this great—even inspired—human interest story to a carefully marshaled argument between various animal lovers and the city, state and federal departments which regulate them. This wasn't *The New York Times Magazine* you were writing for, Robert! Who do you think reads *New York Magazine*? Do you? It's much too thoughtful and considered for them. Plus it's 25 pages long, for God's sake! What is that, 8,000 words or so? That's half their damn magazine! What were you thinking? They have to have room for advertising, don't they? That's how they make their revenue. This is capitalism, buddy. Don't forget."

So that's how they came to be singing, and after thirty-five minutes of belting out the blues and its opposites, Robert slumped back into his favorite easy chair (the only one in Mortimer's tidy, beautifully decorated but small apartment) and stared into the middle distance.

"Look," said Mortimer finally. "You've fallen on hard times. I get it. We all have them. Remember, as I've told you before, when I first got to New York from Ethiopia I was going into restaurants and stealing the little packages of ketchup they had on the tables because at that moment that was literally all I had to eat. And these are really hard times for everyone, Robert! I was reading recently about the uptick in murders in the City. There were more homicides in the first half of 1972—only two years ago—than at any time in our history! Why do you think that happens? People are up against it, man! Not just you! Remember that the whole damned city recently went bankrupt! And when Abe Beame appealed to the federal government for help, President Ford replied: 'Drop Dead!' Or so the Post reported it. Remember that headline? These are terrible times, Robert! Terrible times."

Robert sighed. "I know, I know! It's stupid for me to feel sorry for myself when everyone else is hurting too. But I oughta be able to figure something out to improve my circumstances, don't you think?"

"Of course! And you will! You will!"

All the way home on the subway, Robert, pleasantly sloshed, was thinking about what Mortimer had said. His friend was good for him, no question. Not only did he talk to him like a Dutch Uncle when he needed it, but he also encouraged Robert in ways that bolstered his confidence. Called him a brilliant writer. *Well, I'm not sure I could ever accept that characterization*, he thought. Brilliant? *Naw, I don't think so, not quite.*

His thoughts meandered on, helped by the booze, the jostling of the train, the late hour. *But I do, I think, have some smarts and some talent. I remember back in high school, when I went cross country to that National High School Institute for Journalism. Northwestern University. "Cherubs" we were called. Now, there were some great writers, I have to admit. Kids from all over the country! Five weeks of writing and rewriting. Like we were all employees of the Chicago Tribune, man, or the Sun-Times! What a panic: Early edition, next edition . . . rewrite the lead as the next piece of news comes in over the wire . . . Rip it up and start again! And no way was I the fastest, or the best. There was that kid from Iowa, for example; he was spectacular! And the other one from . . . where was it? . . . Boston? Yeah, Ronald Something. And the girls, also! Two I remember especially. Those guys were the prize winners for writing, not me. Oh, I wasn't forgotten, I won the Boys' Tennis Championship . . . and the Best Dancer Award. But best writer? No prize at the bottom of the Cracker Jack box on that score. I mean . . . I was good, a helluva lot better than some, but brilliant? I think that's stretching it. Still, I can write. So, one way or another, like Mort says, I've gotta keep plugging. I'm no longer a Russian historian, that's for sure . . . those days are behind me. Forever? Who knows? But write? Yes! That I can do and will do! Not just poetry either. But short stories, maybe even novels . That's what I want. That's what I really, really want.*

Later he would wonder whether it was just coincidence that the very next Saturday morning he received a phone call from C.K. O'Connor.

"Robert, good morning! How are you? C.K. here. Long time no see. Listen, dear heart, I would like to invite you to dine with me at twelve-noon today at a brand new restaurant called *Memories*. Forty-fourth Street between Fifth and Sixth. Very *Chi-Chi*. And on me."

"Really? You're inviting me to lunch? What did I do to deserve this? I haven't won the Pulitzer Prize or something, have I?"

"Not yet you haven't. At least not that I know of. So. Can you make it? Say yes, Big Guy!"

"Hmm. Must admit I'm still suspicious. Have you inherited a bundle from a rich uncle or something?"

"Something. My little secret until you get here, okay? Can you make it?"

"Well. Let me consult my social calendar. Let's see . . . perhaps I can put that meeting off 'til later today . . . and . . . yes, that one I can move to next week. Let me think a moment . . . . Oh! You know what? By Golly, I believe. . . if I shuffle my appointments a trifle, I just might be able to make it, C.K."

"Busy boy, these days, eh?"

"C.K., I wouldn't know a social calendar if it hit me on the head. Of course I can make it! A free meal! Are you kidding? Looking forward. Especially if it's on your rich uncle."

"Terrific! See you at high noon. Don't disappoint me now."

She was seated at a large round table set just for two in the very heart of the restaurant when he arrived, white table-cloth and fancy cutlery surrounding her, a blue Daquiri in front of her, long red tresses flaming out around her. She lifted her drink in greeting the moment he walked into the place. He smiled and once arrived at her table, kissed her on both cheeks. As soon as he was seated, she piped up.

"Great to see you, my dear friend. You're looking good!"

"Well, thank you, ma'am! You're not so bad yourself!"

"A drink, perhaps?"

"Oh, sure. Something tall, cold and full of gin."

She laughed and signaled the waiter, who took his drink order, bowed, and vanished.

"Wow! I feel like I'm at the *Four Seasons* or someplace. This is really something. But how did you become flush enough to treat me to lunch?"

She squealed in delight but turned an imaginary key in her lips, clearly determined to reveal nothing until the waiter returned with his drink. When they'd clinked glasses and each taken a sip, she began.

"Well, Bobby boy, I've just been appointed Executive Editor of a new spin-off of *Clubhouse Magazine*. A brand-new venture called *Infinite Varieties*. Part of Bob Maccione's publishing empire. It's a monthly—format about the size of *Reader's Digest*—devoted to short stories with decidedly sexual themes. All varieties, hence, the name. And I'd like to include you in my harem. What do you say?"

"Wow! Congratulations. For sure. But did you just say you wanted me in your harem?"

She positively glowed. "My retinue of writers, yes." She fished in a large handbag. "I have a couple of issues here for you to ponder."

"Sexual themes, you say?"

"Yes! You know Bob Maccione's magazine, *Clubhouse*, I'm sure?"

'Of course."

Next to *Playboy*, *Clubhouse* was the most famous magazine of its kind. It was, he was quite sure, highly profitable. But how, he wondered, did C.K. land such a job? Last time he'd seen her, she was as broke as he was, and living in the Hotel Opera. Had Bob Maccione somehow become one of "her men"? He decided not to ask.

"So, when did this happen? When did you become editor of . . . *Infinite Varieties*?"

"Couple of months ago, my friend. And since you're one of my favorite writers, I couldn't wait to contact you."

He raised his glass again and saluted her. "Congrats,

again, C. K. And thanks for thinking of me. But—goodness—this is going to take some getting used to."

His mind was buzzing like a hive of honeybees gathering pollen. *Porn.* She was asking him to write porn for money. Well, he had nothing *against* porn, did he? Certainly, he'd read a bit. He used to have a small collection of racy novels when he was in his early twenties. One summer when he'd been teaching at that small liberal arts college on the West Coast, he'd decided to spend two months near the UC Berkeley campus in California, and had sublet his apartment in the small Washington town where he taught to four Southern college boys who'd arrived in town from North Carolina to work the pea harvest. They'd seemed like nice kids, much like the students he taught, so he'd trusted them. When he returned at summer's end, alas, he found they'd absconded with every sexy title in his library. *Fanny Hill. A Man with a Maid. My Secret Life.* On and on. And of course, included in their haul were major modern writers famous for the "erotica" passages in their works — D. H. Lawrence, Vladimir Nabokov, Henry Miller among them. He'd particularly mourned the copy of *Tropic of Cancer* he'd been gifted some years earlier by a young woman who'd smuggled it back from Paris in the bottom of her suitcase.

"I'm guessing you don't have anything against erotic writing, do you?"

"Hardly. Quite the contrary. I'm curious, though. What prompted Maccione to start this particular venture?"

"My guess is he's made so much money with *Clubhouse* that he needs a losing venture to give him a tax write-off. Hence his generosity, like my expense account."

"Now that's an income tax problem I'm pretty certain I'll never experience. So tell me, Ms. Newly Crowned Executive Editor of *Infinite Variety*, what kind of money are you allowed to distribute to the inhabitants of this. . .retinue of yours? Or 'harem', as you prefer to call it."

"A thousand bucks a story."

Robert's eyebrows shot up. "A thousand dollars?"

"Yep. No matter which variety of sex you choose to write about. Open Marriage. Oral. Bondage. Massage. Threesomes. Gay Sex. Incest. Exhibitionism. Voyeurism. Whatever turns you on."

He laughed. "A thousand bucks *for one story?* I have to say, that's certainly tempting!"

"We think it's generous enough to attract good writers. So. Are you in?"

Robert looked away a moment. He was amazed. It was not what he'd hoped eventually to write, of course. But at this point in his life, earning money was everything. A story of this nature, eschewing the niceties of character development, psychological realism and serious intent, shouldn't take much of that precious time, especially with an already defined theme. He might even begin to pay down his mounting credit card debt, with its maddeningly usurious interest rates! So how could he refuse? Smiling, he lifted his glass once again.

"Count me in, C.K. And thank you for the opportunity."

"Happy to have you aboard, matey. Welcome to Bob Maccione's empire."

Robert shook his head and laughed. "Who would've thought? Damn, C. K. You sound like you're right in your métier. This is a perfect job for you. So how about "massage"? Is that a theme I can do a story on for the next issue?"

"You got it, bro. But make it sexy, right?"

"Understood."

At the end of their meal—tempted though he was—Robert demurred when she suggested a dessert that would have stuffed him with more calories than he normally ingested in a week. At last, wiping his mouth and tossing his napkin on the table, he stood and smiled. She circled the table and gave him a hug and a juicy kiss.

"This was wonderful, C. K.," he said. "Thanks for the meal and the opportunity."

"No problem, pet. I'll send you a contract as soon as I get back to my office. And I'll look for your story in the mail."

ROOMMATES

ROBERT FAIRWEATHER HAD not had a roommate since he was a sophomore in college. While a freshman, he'd boarded at Mama O'Doyle's Rooming House—breakfast and dinner included—in the neighborhood that had yet to be called Watts. He and his five fellow boarders were all attending the University of Southern California. "My boys," as Mama O'Doyle referred to them. But the following year a student older by one year than he—a Jewish religion major named Jason Feuerbach (whom he'd met while having coffee and reviewing his class notes at a local diner) asked if he'd like to share an apartment and he'd agreed. Same money, less fuss, more time to read. Robert had done most of the cooking, based on recipes he'd cribbed from his mom, though twice a month Jason's lawyer mother had invited the two of them to dinner at her house. That year proved interesting, first because Jason was smart, thoughtful and intellectually alive—the main reason Robert had said yes—and second because he owned a Mercedes Benz diesel two-door sedan which ferried the two of them all over Southern California. A year further on, however, after Jason had found a girlfriend and wanted to move in with her, Robert had relocated to a kind of "student collective" (again, all males) that managed to carve the rent up through common agreement that each would perform a share of the household chores. (Robert was tasked with washing the breakfast dishes and excommunicating the trash.)

This did not mean that from then to now, Robert had never shared a household with another person. In fact, he'd been married twice, once in early grad school days at UCLA and once while a young college teacher. And subsequently, he'd cohabited for two years with a still different woman, an artist, while he was completing his PhD at Columbia, that indelible interval being equally divided between one year of bliss and another of utter hell. In fact, several of that lady's paintings (which she'd either denounced or abandoned) still adorned his walls.

But now—in these post-teaching days which he'd been flung into willy-nilly during the seventies—*this* was, as the saying has it, a whole new ball of wax. Or a horse of a different color. Or a different (distinctive? atypical?) kettle of fish. Robert groaned aloud as each familiar bromide stormed his brain and just as rapidly withdrew.

No, he concluded, staring hard at the figures he'd scribbled on his yellow pad, this time it wasn't romance, or sex, or companionship, or even a yen for a bit of conversation that was the driver of the decision he seemed poised to make. It was money.

Sitting at the kitchen table, he reviewed his household budget. Money for rent. Money for eats. Money for the subway. Money for laundry. Money to replace the one or two threadbare shirts that hid out in his closet (as well as the decomposing underwear in his bureau). Money for cigarettes. (Note to self: *nasty habit, must get rid of it.*) Money for the occasional glass of beer or wine or—maybe once in a blue moon—something stronger. He tried to stay within strict guidelines, but really? A movie once in a while would be welcome, would it not? And has asking someone out on a date now and then been relegated to a distant memory? Was his sex life doomed to extinction?

He sighed again. The balances on all three credit cards, despite how sparingly he tried to use each, were beginning to alarm him as well. Okay. So there was a reason *rent* was the *universal first item* on everyone's household budget! Until he could find a way to earn more money, the surest way to stay afloat was to find someone to share that cost.

I. Ileana

When the doorbell rang to signal what was almost certain to be the first candidate to become his roommate, he had no idea what to expect. Male? Female? Smoker? Non-smoker? American? Foreigner? He'd been intentionally vague in his weekend ad in the *Village Voice*. (He'd splurged, paying for the advertisement with his Amex Card.) But whatever his expectations might have been, they were wrong.

A woman in her mid-twenties stood before him, big blue eyes and medium-length blonde hair, wearing a pale green halter top that kept from view only the lower portion of her breasts. The upper reaches, whose quivering afforded the occasional glimpse of a coral nipple, seemed to have lives of their own. She wore an open, cream-colored linen duster and, underneath, a mauve mini-skirt.

"Hi," she said. "I'm Ileana." She smiled warmly.

"Ah!" said Robert, straightening his posture and putting himself on amber alert. "Pleased to meet you, Ileana. I'm Robert. Yes, yes! Please come in. You're my very first applicant."

He ushered her through the small foyer into the living room and seated himself on his daybed, which he'd spread for the occasion with a nice blue cotton coverlet, spotted with yellow and blue flowers. (It was actually a tablecloth). He invited her to sit down beside him, and she did so, never taking her eyes from his.

"Well, this is it," he said, as she shrugged off her wrapper and folded it neatly beside her. "This is the living room . . . obviously . . . and I'll . . . uh . . . show you the bedroom in a minute or two. As you might gather, it's a pretty large one-bedroom apartment."

Her eyes swept in a half circle, taking in the paintings, the black bookcases, the chess set on the table in front of them, the orange sling chair together with its ottoman, which perched just under the huge plate-glass windows.

"We're close to downtown Brooklyn. I mean . . . actually, this *is* downtown Brooklyn. You'll notice there's a very nice view of the Manhattan Bridge through those windows."

He found himself not looking at the bridge, but at her slender legs in their sheer taupe nylons.

"You have a lot of books!" she exclaimed.

He wondered, from her point of view, was that a good thing or a bad thing?

"Uh, yes. Lots of books. Well, up until recently I taught at the college right across the street. Brooklyn Quintessential University. BQU? This building is owned by them, has a lot of other professors in it as well. I've been living here by myself for . . . some years now. But since I'm no longer teaching, I find myself a little strapped for cash, so that's why I'm in need of someone to share the apartment and the rent. So, tell me, Ileana—uh—where do you live now? And do you live alone?"

She was still looking around. It seemed to him she was favorably impressed.

"Oh. Well, I just arrived in town a couple of weeks ago. And where I'm staying is very temporary. So, I need to find something soon. And, yes, I am alone. And I'm working. And earning . . . pretty good money."

"I see. That's good, that's good. Well, there's quite a lot of room here, I think you'll agree. I plan to split the rent evenly between us. And you'd have access to the kitchen, of course. You can cook here or not, as you prefer. You'd be free to use my plates, pots, pans and so on, just so long as you wash everything you use, of course."

He told her what her share would be of the monthly cost. She didn't blanch.

"Here," he said, as she continued to swivel left and right to take it in. "Let me show you the rest."

He walked her through the kitchen, the dining area, then the bathroom. Wanting to guide her by touching her slender waist. But not. But not. Finally, down the hall and into the bedroom.

"This is where you'd sleep," he said. "The bed is yours. In fact, this room would be all yours. I'm planning to sleep on the daybed in the living room.

"And that's it," he said finally, once she'd admired the ample closet space, and peeked out the window at Myrtle Avenue. "I'll still need to keep a few things in the closet here, but I'd . . . uh . . . of course knock before I came in. I'm sure we can work that out."

She nodded. And smiled.

He led her back to the living room, where they resumed seating. He did his best to avoid staring at her breasts. Was it just his imagination that they seemed . . . so animated? Almost to have a life of their own?

He cleared his throat. "So . . . what do you do, Ileana? I believe you said you had a job, correct?"

She smiled, turned her attention to the windows, then the paintings.

"Well, I turn tricks now and then," she said.

Robert stopped breathing. Almost. Well, there it was then. It all made sense somehow. He chuckled very softly, shook his head and looked away a moment. Nothing is simple, is it?

"I've nothing against that line of work, of course," he said at last. "But . . . I couldn't have you doing anything like that here."

"Oh, no! Of course not! This would be where I live, not where I work. I'm already working, at a house in midtown. That's where I'm sleeping too at the moment, but it's just temporary. I only moved here from Las Vegas two weeks ago."

"Vegas, you say?"

"Yes. That's where I'm from. I mainly came to New York to earn some money to get my teeth fixed." She obligingly opened her mouth and pulled her lower lip down, leaning closer to him so he could get a good look. He found himself looking past her mouth to the jiggling of her torso. To him, the teeth didn't even look that bad.

"Ah." He cleared his throat. "I see."

He thought a moment. "You know," he said finally, "I've been married a couple of times but I'm single now. I don't suppose there's any chance that you and I . . ."

"Well," she said. "It might be possible, but I'd have to charge you. You're a nice-looking man, but I'm trying to get my teeth fixed. And with what I charge . . . there goes your rent reduction!"

Robert laughed softly. "Of course," he said. "Of course. I understand. You're absolutely right. And cutting my rent is exactly why I'm doing this in the first place. Yes. Of course. Well . . . there you are, then. Ileana, if you want it, the share is yours. Are you agreed?"

"Wonderful!" she said.

He stuck out his hand and they shook.

"I'll see you Wednesday night then," she said. "And here's my share of this month's rent right now. Is that okay?" She opened her purse, removed a wad of cash, and counted out the bills.

"I very much appreciate that," he said. "So, it's all settled then! I'll have a key made for you and I'll see you Wednesday evening. Looking forward to it. You're a charming young woman, Ileana. Welcome to Brooklyn!"

The sexual frisson (or three-bell alarm) that accompanied the arrival of Ms. Ileana Kordon as Robert's first roommate of the modern era was eventually diffused, helped in no small measure by how seldom he saw her. Once she'd settled in, their hours were quite different. She tended to arrive back at the apartment late in the evening or early in the morning when he'd been long ensnared by the covers of his daybed. She'd let herself in quietly and retire to her room with no alarming clang or clatter of dishes from the kitchen and was soundly asleep in her room when he departed in the morning after a shower, a quick breakfast and departure to his 9-5 employment. Consequently, they saw each other only rarely. (He did peek in on her one morning soon after her arrival, assuring himself he was doing so only to determine that she was actually there) and found that she slept asprawl of the bed and was snoring peacefully. Unfortunately, for whatever "peeping-tom" inclinations informed his gesture, the bedclothes gave adequate cover to her body.

They held brief conversations occasionally, usually on Saturday mornings before she left for her dental appointments. (She'd been deadly serious about having her teeth fixed; by the end of their association as roommates she would often attempt to dazzle him with her smile.)

In short, she proved an affable roommate, though Robert found her a curiosity. She was nobody's fool. On the one hand, a professional. In firm control. At the same time, however, she radiated an innocence, a guilelessness. No hardened demeanor, not a trace of cynicism.

Another dimension surprised him as well. Very soon after she moved in, she brought back to the apartment a potted plant, placed it on the kitchen table and continued to nurture it. Quite lovingly. Only the plant was not a camellia, nor a daisy, nor a dahlia, nor a chrysanthemum, nor an orchid. It was a tiny bush of flame-red Scotch Bonnet peppers, which she gleefully described to Robert as "one hundred times hotter than a jalapeño." Since she never cooked, it was unclear what sparked her interest, but her infatuation was intense. Though he failed to understand that particular passion, he was moved when some months later, as she left New York, she decided to leave behind the plant as a gift to him, and he treasured it for some time thereafter.

In one of their infrequent exchanges, she announced, quite out of the blue, "I'm getting fucked in the ass a lot lately."

"Oh?" said Robert, unsure where this might be going. After a distinct interval, he said, "Does that mean you prefer it that way?"

"Not particularly. Just less bother. The johns can't even tell."

"Really?"

"Gospel. So long as you're the one who puts it in, they don't even know. And it's a lot less cleanup and stuff."

And that was that.

Six months into their association, and a mere two months before she left to return to Vegas—all dental work completed—she had a visitor.

"Robert, this is Dave," she said. "He just flew in from Las Vegas to see how I was doing. He and Cheryl are my handlers. I lived with them in Vegas. Real sweet couple. I've known them my whole professional life."

They shook hands. He was short, slim, affable, low-key, straightforward. A sun-darkened man with wavy black hair flecked with grey. He wore jeans and a pullover.

"Pleased to meetcha," Dave said. "Had a nice flight. Better weather here than I expected."

"Yes, it has been nice lately. Good to meet you, Dave."

Robert decided Dave had a very pleasant smile.

"I've known Dave and Cheryl since I was a girl," said Ileana. "They introduced me to the business. Wonderful people. Like an aunt and uncle I never had. They look out for me."

Robert decided to make coffee for the three of them.

While doing so, he said: "That's very important, I would imagine. Nice to know they've got your back, right?"

In his mind Robert was saying, *Not a pimp. A handler. Okay. Was she being 'handled,' even here? How much of her money does she get to keep?*

And, of course, that evening, Dave slept in the other room—Robert's old bedroom—with Ileana. *Was that kosher?* he wondered. *What did the wife think?* He felt a twinge of jealousy.

As he left for work that morning, already aware Dave would be returning to Vegas that afternoon, Robert thought, *Actually, he really does seem like a nice guy. So. It's*

a great big, complicated world out there, Robert. Who knows
which end is up?

II. RALPH

There were three other roommates during the years that
Robert needed to split the rent on his apartment. Two of
those—Terry Sheridan and Jack Livermore—stayed but a
little while and left few enduring impressions. Terry was a
tall, even-featured, soft-bearded young fellow who didn't
talk much (possibly because he didn't know much) but
was apparently quite attractive to women. On two separate Sunday mornings, a few weeks apart, Robert awoke
to find an attractive younger woman pacing back and
forth in his living room, either fully or partially dressed,
having awakened before her lothario and now eager to get
on with the rest of her day but believing it highly inap-
propriate to quit the premises unaccompanied. Jack, on
the other hand, was a younger and more helter-skelter
specimen than Terry—he couldn't have been more than
twenty—with restless blue eyes, stringy blonde hair down
to his shoulders, and a simmering anger that was barely
suppressed. He slammed cupboard doors, let out oaths at
odd moments, and left tracks out of the bathroom after his
showers, but Robert finally found it necessary to evict him
only after being awakened by a clattering racket outside

in the BQU Towers parking lot. He looked down twelve floors to discover his roommate indiscriminately kicking garbage cans all over the tarmac.

Ralph Katorz, on the other hand—the last roommate to share the apartment with Robert—stayed for over a year and was, in Robert's opinion, by many kilometers the most interesting. A high-school dropout, a decade or so older than Robert, of medium height, more than a little overweight, with thinning hair, a round face that managed to be both cherubic and sad, he was not particularly good-looking, or even striking, and swarmed with attitudes that struck Robert as more from the street than the classroom. On the other hand, he had a good heart and an easy, self-deprecating humor.

Ralph had no memory of either father or mother. He'd grown up near the railroad tracks in East Lost Angeles. He might even have been a discard—an afterthought—left in a basket or cardboard box on the steps of some church; he couldn't say.

So Ralph was an ill-educated street kid from a busted neighborhood. Having sex when he was ten (so he said), getting into trouble even earlier. He'd known jail, though never prison. During the early part of his youth, he'd fallen into grifting: always a scheme, a ploy, somewhere on the horizon. He remembered combing through dumpsters for letters to find names and addresses which he'd sell to someone who could make use of them for one scheme or another. What had saved him from an even more dodgy and dangerous life, he felt certain, was falling into acting. Once that interest blossomed, it had led him to appear in a variety of local stage productions in LA and surrounding communities, as well as to work as an extra in movies when nothing else was available. He'd come to New York, he told Robert, to write a screen play, its lead character a middle-aged man who repossessed cars. Part of the action of his hoped-for movie took place in New York City.

Robert supposed he felt drawn to Ralph not because of any similarity in their own immediate backgrounds, but because he was something of an urban version, absent the larceny perhaps, of his father. Robert's own dad, growing up in the Oklahoma countryside, had dropped out of school in the fourth grade when his mother died, ridden the rails seeking work during the depression and, despite marrying a woman who had actually finished high school, never shook off his lower-class country background. Whatever the case, Robert grew to like Ralph. They had many a good-natured argument, but over time became what most people would have called . . .pals.

Their first set-to happened over all things French. One morning they were sharing breakfast while listening to the radio. Edith Piaf's distinctive voice came on, singing "*La vie en rose,*" and Ralph said, "Can we catch a different station? I hate Edith Piaf."

"You don't like Edith Piaf! Why on earth is that?"

"I don't like frogs in general."

"Frogs? That's a pretty insulting way to speak about the French, isn't it? Are we back in World War II now?"

"Hey, why not? It's how I feel. "

"Don't you even like French food? Me, I like to cook, and French dishes are among my favorites. I make a great *coq au vin*. And *beef bourguignon*. Even the things I don't cook I enjoy eating. *Cassoulet. Bouillabaisse. Quiche!* And you gotta like chocolate *mousse!*"

"Spare me. I've been to France, and their food is so pretentious and their waiters are all stuck-up. Those fucking waiters think they own the world. If you don't give 'em the tip they think they deserve they look down their noses at you. Like you're supposed to be serving them instead of the other way around."

"Hmm." After a couple of beats, Robert said, "Did you ever think about your last name?"

"What about it?"

"Say it for me."

"You know what it is. Katorz. You have a problem with my name?"

"Not a bit. It's probably Polish in origin but the way it's pronounced is identical to the French word '*Quatorze*,' which means 'Fourteenth.'"

"So? Why would I care about that?"

"Do you know who Louis the Fourteenth was? I just find it a little ironic that your last name is the same as the title of the most famous French king who ever lived. Louis the Fourteenth. Seventeenth Century. The Sun King. And yet you hate the French. Go figure."

"Well, you call it ironic, but I don't care. Moronic is more like it. I still hate the Frogs."

Robert smiled, shrugged his shoulders and dropped the subject.

Among the ways in which Robert benefitted from Ralph's company was by being an occasional passenger in his car, an old but roomy Buick four-door. (His roommate had driven back to New York from LA. And as a perk of now living in BQU Towers, could stash his car free of charge in the university's underground garage.) Their first outing together came when Ralph invited him to a read-through of a play that Ralph hoped to get cast in. The location was in a large town house on the Upper East Side. Robert—who'd had some amateur theatrics in his background—was eager to accept the invitation. It was held in a huge living room packed with about twenty-five or thirty aspirants. At the event, the director, a middle-aged man with straight black hair and glasses, asked Robert if he'd like to read the lines of one of the characters as well (the play had a huge cast). While he had no ambitions to join the cast, he happily agreed. He found the evening quite enjoyable, though they returned late, and he didn't get to bed until after midnight, making him a bit sleepy the next day at work. The reading, unfortunately, did not result in a job for Ralph, and Robert had no idea whether the play was ever performed. He also nurtured the opinion that his own reading of his character in that script had been superior to Ralph's, but he wisely kept that opinion to himself.

On an occasion several weeks later, Ralph, who, seeking female companionship, frequently traipsed off on a Saturday night to some bar or ballroom, asked Robert if he wanted to go along. Robert decided, why not? Wasn't it time, he wondered, to make an effort to break his condition of boring abstinence? Or at least to try? So, he counted his cash and said yes.

As it happened, they both were successful in their quests that evening, discovering two ladies at Roseland (the two were neighbors in Westchester and had journeyed to the dance hall together that evening) who not only enjoyed their two suitors as dance partners but were eager—or at least easily persuaded—to accept their invitation to spend the night together. So Rhonda and Frieda, each a widow, both in their forties, one tall, lanky and prone to giggles—Robert's, the other more portly and eager to chat—Ralph's)—accompanied their new paramours back to Brooklyn. Robert and his overnight mistress spent the night on his daybed's two foam cushions, pushed together and crowded into a captive space on the floor between the living room and the dining alcove. Meanwhile, Ralph and his guest performed their sexual shenanigans in the comfortable (but rented) double bed Robert had once claimed as his own. (Robert, of course, would never relinquish the conviction that both spaces were his by divine right.) Each couple certainly deemed the evening satisfactory as far as it went (so the yelps and moans attested), but none seemed prone to repeat it, and hence it never was. Robert accompanied Ralph as he drove Rhonda and Frieda back to midtown the next day, where the two ladies rescued Rhonda's car from the garage where it had been held captive overnight and, waving merrily goodbye, drove north to Westchester.

Ralph had many more excursions on which Robert did not accompany him and, the next morning over breakfast after one of those a couple of months later, he asked, "Say, Bobby, do you happen to know a C. K. O'Connor?"

Robert put down the fork with which he was about to skewer his last morsel of scrambled eggs and looked at Ralph with suspicion. "This is a joke, right?"

Ralph shook his head, still chewing on a strip of bacon.

"Well, yes, I do," Robert said. "Quite well, as a matter of fact. Don't tell me she was the woman you bedded last night?"

Ralph shook his head and chuckled. "No, no. Not at all," he said. "What I'm saying is that I met and 'bedded'— to use your term—a broad in her forties named Bridget Riley. And she claims to be C. K.'s best friend. I had just mentioned that you and I were roommates, and when she heard your name, that's when she told me."

Robert looked at Ralph with even greater suspicion. "Do you know how unlikely this strikes me? I mean, what are the chances? In a town of seven million people? A few years back I met C.K. at a poetry reading and we did hook up now and then, for a time. I still know her, but now more because she's the editor of Bob Maccione's publication, *Infinite Variety*. So, I see her only whenever I'm in desperate need of dough to ask if she'd like me to write another story for her periodical. I get a thousand bucks a story."

It was Ralph's turn to laugh and shake his head. "Maccione. Same guy who owns *Clubhouse*, right? Must be rich as all get-out, that guy."

"Right. So tell me. How did you meet this . . . Riley woman?"

"Picked her up last night at a bar, went to her place. And get this, she swings both ways. And C. K., in addition to being her buddy, is also her main squeeze."

Robert's eyebrows looked like they were about to be launched into outer space. "No shit?"

"God's honest truth! At least to hear her tell it. Believe me, I couldn't make this up."

"Well, I'll be damned." Robert shook his head slowly back and forth, a puzzled smile on his face, still trying to process the information. Finally, he laughed. "Well, there you go then. I have to say, that part is a surprise. I guess *Infinite Variety* is a fitting name for her publication, right?"

"Damn straight. And you know how I know all this? Or one reason?"

"Tell me."

"Well, I actually have trouble getting it up these days. So I've taken to going down on women a lot and gotten pretty good at it. And that must be what they do, too. Right? I have an experienced tongue by this time and, evidently, that's what Bridget likes best. What they both like."

Robert wadded up his napkin and tossed it in his plate. "Are you seeing this lady again?"

"Yep. You bet. Next Saturday."

"Well, please pass along my regards to C. K. while you're at it. Tell her I'll be calling her soon. Okay?"

At long last, Ralph's screenplay was finished. He'd worked rather tirelessly, Robert thought, plugging away over the last year at his Remington portable. Hunt and peck, hunt and peck. But over time, it got done. Robert noticed the script one Saturday morning on the kitchen table where Ralph's ypewriter usually sat. Where Ralph had disappeared to so early, he'd no idea, but he picked it up and began thumbing through its pages.

He soon brewed coffee and sat down on his daybed to read further. He slid the chess board aside to give himself room to read it more comfortably. And—somewhat to his surprise—found he quite liked it. It struck him as smart, moved well, and he found the scenes terse and arresting.

Ralph clearly knew how to create tension, understood suspense. Robert could visualize the scenes as he read. He also found the characters likable, even compelling. The central character was, unsurprisingly, Robert's roommate. The spitting image: Ralph in all his commonplace glory. His physical description, his mannerisms, his lingo. His profession was, of course, he repossessed cars. There was a love interest as well, which began with a woman whose '71 Pontiac he was attempting to make off with. She interrupted him and screamed. She railed, begged, cried. Eventually invited him into her house for coffee. This proved a much more romantic encounter than Robert had expected. Their sex scenes were surprisingly circumspect. Through parts of the story, the protagonist worked with a sidekick. And no (Robert was relieved to find), the sidekick was nothing like him.

When he'd finally finished—several hours, a couple of snacks, and three cups of coffee later—he was impressed. He decided it ought to make an entertaining movie. He felt very happy for Ralph and shared that information the moment his roommate walked through the door in the late afternoon, both arms full of large grocery bags, which he'd generously bought to restock Robert's cupboards, a kind of going-away present.

After they'd unloaded the groceries they returned to the living room, where Ralph sat in the sling chair while Robert took his accustomed spot on the daybed.

"Thanks for what you said there, Bobby boy. About the script and all. I appreciate that, especially coming from you. My time here is almost up, you know. I accomplished what I came here to do."

"You certainly did, and I'm proud of you, Ralphie. I've enjoyed having you here. You've been a real pal. So, it's back to LA soon, is it?"

"Yeah, back to La La Land. Hope I can sell the damn thing. In Hollywood it's always a hundred-to-one shot, no matter who you know. I'm hoping to play the lead, you understand, if they'll let me. If anybody sees what I see and wants to make the goddamned thing."

"They should. They should make it. I'd certainly go to see it. Maybe you should take Bridget back to LA with you to play the female lead?"

He laughed. "Naw, naw. That's done. Nice while it lasted, though. I've had a good time here."

"Same goes for me, Ralphie. It's been really nice knowing you."

"Well, we can stay in touch. By the way, I'm out of savings now—just about enough to get me back to the other coast—so I'll need to get something going as soon as I get back."

"Anything in mind?"

"Yes, as a matter of fact. Been working it out with a friend of mine in LA. Guy I've worked with some before. Real nice plan, I think."

"Sounds good. Care to share?"

"So, everyone wants to write a song, right? Everybody thinks they have at least one song in them. If only there were some way to record it, get somebody interested. And that's what me and my friend are planning to do. We got it all worked out, see? People will write their songs—both music and lyrics—then send them to us. We'll record it, send 'em a record, and we'll also share it with the major radio stations so they can play it on air and make our customers stars overnight. Good plan, right? Of course, they pay a fee up front for our doing all this."

"Hmm. Isn't it expensive to do those recordings?"

"Hardly at all. LA is like New York: musicians a dime a dozen. All waiting around for some gig or another. So we gather up these dudes— for *scale*, mind you—then rent a studio and record as many as ten records in one session. Then we mail 'em a copy of their record, and also promise to send it around to various disc jockeys, which we do. All this for a fixed price. Twenty-five hundred bucks. Up front. Doesn't cost us that much, so by the time we get a few thousand people signed up we should be makin' good money."

"And these would-be songwriters. They're expecting you can actually make their song a hit?"

"We paint it as rosy as we can, of course . . . . I mean, it could happen, right? You never know."

"What are the chances that those disc jockeys you send it to will actually play their song on the air?"

"Slim to none. The reality is they'll just unwrap it and toss it in the crapper. No disc jockey plays an unknown record unless someone with real juice leans on 'em hard. Just doesn't happen."

"So it's kind of a scam, right? You're selling them a pipe dream for their $2,500?"

"Well, they do get a record out of it. With some cat singing to the music of an actual band. So that's worth something."

Ralph paused a moment while Robert pondered his description.

"So what we need," Ralph continued, "is to make it known, to entice people to write to us and send their checks. That's where you might come in. You could set up a post office box downtown in the Wall Street area. Then we'd have an impressive address in the Big Apple, right? Home of Tin Pan Alley. Every once in a while, you'd collect the mail and forward it to us. Not much work and you'd get a cut, of course. We'd make it worth your while."

Robert laughed gently and shook his head. "Ralph, forgive me, but I don't think so. It's just not my scene, I'm afraid. I love your screenplay and I wish you luck with it. And I've really enjoyed having you around this last year or so. But what you're planning, I'm afraid I really wouldn't want any part of."

His roommate shrugged and threw up his hands. He smiled. "Well, I tried anyway."

And a year after that conversation, Robert would learn from a letter that his friend had indeed managed to set up the business they'd discussed and was busy recording songs. And a few years after that he also learned, sadly, that Hollywood did make a movie called "Repo Man," but it bore no correspondence to the script Ralph had been working on.

The discussion about Ralph's plans for his new LA venture was almost the last time they talked. The next day, a Sunday—all in preparation for leaving—Ralph was cleaning out the bedroom that had been home base to him for over a year. Robert could hear him whistling as he wielded the small vacuum cleaner. All of a sudden, the noise stopped, and Ralph came gleefully sashaying down the hall holding something in his hand.

"I think this is your souvenir, not mine," he grinned. "Found them way under the bed."

Panties? Robert delicately took them between two fingers and stared. Small, white, cotton. Obviously belonging to someone he'd once known. How long ago? He laughed and shook his head.

"No idea," he said. "An artifact from Ancient History. Only wish I could remember whose they were."

THE CHIMERA

F A FA, ZIPPITY DAH. WHATEVER, WHATEVER, FOREVER, FOREVER. WHAT TO DO NOW? GROW BIG, GROW LONG; SING A GOOD SONG! SONG ONE, SONG TWO, WHAT DID YOU DO? CAN'T THINK OF A THING TO SAY. WHAT A GROSS FUCKING DAY. ETC., ETC., ETC. OH! CAN ONE RHYME SOMETHING WITH ETCETERA? NOT A THING. NOT A BLOODY DAMNED THING. ETC. IS A FREAKY DARK CORNER, WHERE NO RHYMES GROW. ETC, ETC, ETC.

All morning Robert Fairweather had been doodling at his typewriter, high in the US Customs and Marketing Federal Bank at One CMFB Plaza, the sixty-story head-quarters building in lower Manhattan whose out-front sculpture looked to most people like a thoroughly squeezed wad of toothpaste with a black thread running through it. He'd been typing whatever came into his head, trying to get himself loosened up. Advised by his bosses—not the ones at Miss Susan's Spectacular Temps, which *was* who paid him—but the ones at CMFB's International Department, which is where he'd been assigned for the last few months: "Feel free to type whatever you want when the numbers haven't come in yet, as long as you zero in on them the moment our managers bring them to you."

So far they'd seemed pleased by his work.

But his fingers interrupted themselves a moment when he overheard the conversation through the open door of Frank Gross's corner office.

"Not a bad idea," bellowed Frank, in his gruff yet genial managerial voice. "Not bad at all. We spend a lot of money getting our monthly report printed on the outside. Every month, and we only make, what, sixty copies? Ron, why don't you investigate the cost of doing it in-house? A quick and dirty cost/benefits analysis, hey? And show me the options on Friday. *Capiche?*"

Ron Harrelson, Manager of the Western Hemisphere Group, left Frank's office smiling, looking?? quite pleased with himself.

Fifty-two seconds later, having given the matter at least half-a-minute's thought, Robert left his chair and his two pages of useless doodles. Circling the floor past four people hard at work on what looked like portfolios of double-entry bookkeeping he entered Frank's open door.

Frank leaned back in his swivel chair and smiled. "How's it goin', Bobby? Are you bored silly? We'll probably have some numbers by late afternoon. Might be an opportunity for some overtime."

"Actually, I couldn't help overhearing your conversation with Mr. Harrelson, Mr. Gross. Are you saying CMFB might decide to buy a printing press to run off the Monthly Report? That means you'll need someone to operate it, right? A printer? I think I'd like to apply for that job."

For more than a year now Robert had made his living as a typist. Maybe it was time for a change?

Two months later, Robert was standing beside an offset printing press, watching with a satisfaction mixed with disgruntlement as it pumped the requisite sixty copies into the receiving bins. Pages that only a few months ago he'd been decorating with numbers himself, on an office typewriter. Once he'd started the machine, inked it up, inserted the master onto the silver drum and flipped the switch, it was capable of operating without him. Until, of course, a particular page had all its copies made and it was time to insert a new master. He actually created those masters as well, on a different machine, which occupied a separate space in his small office, taking the freshly typed and sequentially numbered copies he'd been given and using them to produce, after the press had been properly inked, the finished report. There was also the cover and the binding—assembled by another, much smaller device—which he also operated. When things worked properly, he found this job far more satisfying than typing.

For the most part the equipment worked well enough, though not flawlessly. Occasionally pages would get sent up the movable ramp on a slight angle and hang up in the bins, requiring the press to be switched off and the bins cleared, which took time and was messy. Other times, if a ream of paper's weave ran crossways, the collator would hang up midway along its programmed arc, and the copies wouldn't go into the bins at all, causing a bottleneck that needed to be cleared and a problem that needed to be solved. Usually that meant starting over, this time reattaching the masters by their edges rather than their tops and readjusting the feeder tray to send the paper in sideways. Truth be told, he'd already begun to yearn for a more sophisticated piece of machinery.

Early one Monday morning, Frank showed up outside Robert's office door, surprising him in the midst of a run.

"Hey, Bobby, everything going okay?"

Robert smiled and, as soon as the page he was running was in the bins, shut down the machine. "Hey yourself, Frank. Pretty well, I think. For the most part."

Frank narrowed his eyes. "For the most part? Are you hinting there's a problem, Bobby? Equipment not performing up to your expectations?" He continued to stand there, lounging his big body against the door jamb. Robert thought he looked rather like a framed photograph, almost a silhouette, with the big picture window in the hallway behind him.

Robert shrugged. "Oh, a few problems, I guess. It's neither the fastest nor the best machine overall, I think. Not as efficient as it could be. Makes for some delays now and then. Still, I certainly prefer it to typing!"

Frank looked thoughtful. "Interested in efficiency, are you? Well, I know from your background you've got some smarts. So, tell me, what would you change?"

"Oh! Well, off the top of my head, I'm not sure. I've been looking at the brochures they keep mailing to me. Not sure how the word gets around."

"Well, I tell you what. You're the one who's handling this equipment, so that makes you the expert. Why don't you do me a cost/benefits analysis and let me know what our options are?"

"Oh! Okay. Yeah, I guess I can do that."

"Good! Let me know in a few days. I'll look it over, see what we can do."

That said, he smiled and departed the doorway for his corner office, just down the hall. The whole department—greatly expanded—was on a different floor now, up a couple from where they'd been before. Only one floor down from where the honchos, the EVPs and the head man himself, were. Robert had been there once, to deliver an envelope to the CEO's secretary—back in the days when he was just a typist—and had swooned over all the modern, abstract art that decorated the walls, of a quality that rivaled any gallery he'd ever been in. Now all the regional outfits—North America, South America, Western Hemisphere, Middle East, and Europe, or at least their financial aspects—had been consolidated under Frank's leadership. His title was now SVP, Senior Vice President, and his large corner office even had a separate, smaller office just outside of it, with a desk of its own. So far unoccupied.

Robert stood for a moment, ruminating. So how did one do a cost/benefits analysis? He'd never seen the one that produced the equipment he was now working with. Oh, well. He'd figure it out, he told himself. He resumed his position at the press and flipped the switch.

And two months after that, things had changed dramatically again. Burning the midnight oil, Robert had completed the c/b analysis in four days, after consulting with Thomas Foyle, a first-rate accountant he'd befriended who'd been with CMFB for forty years. He thought Tom was amazing. He'd come to CMFB right out of high school, often described himself as "shanty Irish," and had, over time, risen to 2nd Vice President. And when it came to numbers, Tom was something of a wunderkind. He played an adding machine like a piano piece by Rachmaninoff. Robert had in fact, in an earlier month, penned a small, humorous poem about him, called "Locked in a Room Full of Numbers with Thomas Foyle ."

And Tom had shown him exactly what to do. "First you break the numbers down to their lowest common denominator," he said. "How many sheets do you produce for how many pennies? With this equipment and that? Then you factor in how much time is spent in producing how much at what cost." He'd done a dry run with one set of numbers Tom had shown him, then researched several other brands and types of equipment and written it up as a comparative report, with an introduction and conclusion. Five pages. After Tom had reviewed it, he'd passed it along to Frank and—a week later—Frank had called him into his corner office and closed the door.

"Bobby, I think you're wasting your time as a printer," he said. "This analysis is first-rate stuff. How many had you done before?"

Robert shrugged. "This is the first. But I had a lot of help from Thomas Foyle."

"Good man, Thomas. But it's how fast you learn that's the question. There's no doubt in my mind that if you took banking seriously, you could become a star. So that's what I'm going to suggest to you. I want you to go home tonight and think about it. In fact, why don't you have dinner with me tomorrow night down at the South Street Seaport? We can discuss your possible career over a plate of scallops and a couple of martinis. Sound like a plan?"

And the next evening, Frank had groomed him, sweet-talked him further.

Robert had been reluctant at first. "I've never really thought of myself as a numbers man," he'd told Frank.

"Banking and Finance isn't just numbers," Frank had said. "It's concepts. Including concepts that haven't even been invented yet. You should think about what concepts you're interested in that might be favorably applied to the banking industry as a whole. You said you were interested in efficiency, for example. Well, there you go. There's plenty of room in this outfit for someone who thinks like that. Banking, like everything else, is continually evolving."

He added, "And over time, you'd certainly be earning more than you are now, or ever did as an academic."

The banker paused long enough to take a sip of his martini. "There are programs you can go into, if you take it seriously. We could send you back to school to take a banking course from Baruch or Stern School of Business or wherever. It'd cost a little, but we could arrange a loan you could pay back over time."

Robert tried to keep from blanching. He still owed Columbia University about $6,000, fortunately deferred for ten years. But somewhere down the road . . . . He took a sip of his martini and smiled politely.

"But if you're tired of formal schooling—I know you already have a PhD—I can show you the ropes myself, maybe send you to a course here and there—over at the world Trade Center, for example—to catch up on some particular ideas. One possibility, as a matter of fact, now that I've acquired a bit more clout in the bank with the expansion of my Office of Financial Services, is to become my Executive Assistant and sit right outside my office door. You'd get a real taste of how things are done. Learning on the job. How would you feel about that?"

It was a week before he knew how he felt about that. He'd talked to his best friend, Mortimer Adams, he'd talked to a few others, he'd sat up nights in his Brooklyn apartment and thought about it some more. But after that week was out—ignoring the deep sigh in his soul—Robert found himself shaking hands over exactly the position Frank had suggested, in that vacant space right outside his office. Another body would be operating the new printing equipment he'd asked for. After two weeks of training the new guy, Robert found himself, albeit with a full flock of butterflies in his stomach, knocking on the door of Frank's office in a suit and tie he hadn't worn since his teaching days, and clutching his long-unused briefcase.

That first morning, unsurprisingly, was a little bewildering, since he had very little idea what he'd be asked to do. Was he a secretary? A gofer? What? But even before he settled those questions, there was something more immediate. Right after he'd endured Frank's, "Welcome aboard, I'm very busy right now, but I'll get back to you before the morning's out; meanwhile just sit there and get adjusted to the space," even before he'd traveled two yards outside the office door, feeling rather like he'd just been tossed over the boss man's shoulder into a carpeted dumpster, he felt the need to stick his head back in again.

"Frank, sorry to bother you, but I've no place to sit. There's no chair at this desk."

"Ah. There are folding chairs in the closet just down the hall. What we use when we have extra guests. That'll have to do for now. Then later I'll teach you how to do a midnight requisition."

Thus it was that, after gathering a chair from the hallway closet Frank had directed him towards, Robert placed it behind his new desk and took a seat, just as Frank shot out of his office, still stuffing papers into his briefcase, and strode off down the hall without another word.

Robert looked at his new desk. There was an inbox and an outbox, both empty. There was a phone, with several buttons, all unlighted. There was a long drawer above his knees and three drawers along the side. All empty. A nice desk blotter, but no yellow pads, no paper, no pencils, no typewriter. There was a new-looking but totally empty wastebasket. That was it. He looked out past the corrugated clear plastic divider which separated him from the broad hallway down which Frank had disappeared and frowned. "What the fuck," he muttered, in a voice he hoped no one could overhear, "is 'a midnight requisition?'"

Over the many weeks he'd now been at CMFB, as typist, as printer, and now as an Executive Assistant, Robert had made cafeteria lunch buddies with several others, all APs, the level below 2VP. Most of those who weren't secretaries were APs. Only a few days into his new position, he was in the midst of biting into a very passable taco prepared by the cafeteria, when one of them, an AP named Willy Loo, remarked casually, "So now you're Frank Gross's hatchet man, eh?"

Robert frowned and lowered his crisp tortilla, trying to keep the lettuce and tomato from spilling out onto his plate. He sat back in his chair. "Willy, no, of course not!" he said. "Why would you say that?"

His other tablemate that midday, a quiet, thoughtful looking chap named Peter Kleindienst, removed his rimless glasses and cleaned them on the sparkling white napkins the cafeteria provided. Then he said, "It's what's going around, Robert. Everyone thinks so."

Robert dropped his hands into his lap and looked around the cafeteria. "Guys, it's not true. Why would people think that? I'm Frank's Executive Assistant. I do whatever he asks me to do. In fact, my duties haven't been completely defined yet. So far, he's asked me to edit a few memos, and once or twice to go around and tell the guys who run the different departments he's in charge of, what he's expecting of them and when he needs it by. I don't have any authority over them or anything. Sometimes I feel more like a secretary than anything else. He told me recently he's speaking next month at some sort of banking conference in Minneapolis and asked can I help him edit the speech. Something that, as a writer, I've had some experience with. In no sense would I call myself a 'hatchet man.' Jeez, guys. That's not it at all."

Willy smiled ruefully and toyed with his burger. "We'll see," he said.

Peter shrugged and picked up his container of yogurt, carefully peeling off the top. "I thought yogurt was supposed to make you lose weight," he said, patting his midriff.

Later, Robert sat at his desk outside Frank's office, as his boss was off at a meeting somewhere. He felt wounded. Hatchet man? What on earth was a hatchet man, anyway? In the several weeks he'd been doing this job, he'd been and was still very unclear about what his duties were. A little bit of this, a little bit of that. He sometimes read the memos that appeared in Frank's inbox (they were put in his inbox first) and, if something occurred to him, made a note about what seemed to him important, without much confidence that it was the case. He was feeling his way. He did have a typewriter now, he no longer doodled, but so far it hadn't got much use. It had shocked him a bit, though he thought he hid it well, when the first day there'd been a meeting in Frank's office, Frank had asked him to go to the urn and get coffee for everyone, all the while insisting, *sotto voce*, that this was "the only time. I'm not planning to turn you into a secretary."

Robert scooted back in his very nice desk chair and

suddenly smiled, remembering. When he'd finally seen Frank, late in that first day of his new position, his boss had said, without any kind of preamble, "OK, here's how you get yourself a chair. This is a big building, Bobby. With a lot of rooms, just on this floor. So I suggest you stay a little late tonight. After everybody's cleared out, or most folks at least, you'll wander around the building, peeking into various empty offices, conference rooms, what have you. Conference rooms are probably best. You're almost certain to find, somewhere, a perfectly good chair that doesn't appear to be used by anyone. So you wheel that chair back along the corridor and over to your desk. It's that simple! What they call a midnight requisition. Just make sure it's after I'm gone. *Capiche*?"

One early afternoon, as Robert was reading a memorandum that had come to Frank from the boys upstairs (the seventeenth floor with all the paintings, where the CEO lurked), Frank entered Robert's cubicle like a small tornado and tossed three stapled pages onto his desk.

"Robert, I need you to revise your job description. It just came back from Personnel. They need more. You need to beef up the description of your duties as my Executive Assistant."
"Oh?"
"Yes."

"Priority?"

"Right away. We need to get it back to Personnel *tout d' suite.*"

"Hey, I didn't know you knew French!"

"Forget French. I mean it, Bobby. Right away."

"Okay. But, Frank, you've never given me a description of my duties, so how am I to know what to put down?"

"Beef it up, Bobby. Make yourself sound more important. You're my Executive Assistant, for God's sake! Not a goddamn secretary."

With that, he vanished into his office and closed the door.

Robert looked out into the hallway and sighed. Several people passed by, presumably on their way to the print shop he used to run—or back from it—but they seemed like ethereal specters whose ghostly movement he barely noticed.

Beef it up? Why was this something he was being asked to do? Presumably Frank knew more about what he wanted from his EA than he did. He'd still not been given a list of tasks. It was all pretty squishy. He did what Frank asked him to do. Yet here he was being told to define what his job was?

He read through the forms in front of him. Yes, he'd written those descriptions himself, because he'd been asked to. Based on the individual tasks required of him thus far. Liaise with the heads of the different banking groups; carry

Frank's orders to them. Remind them of deadlines. Handle correspondence and reports for the Senior Vice President. (Actually, that was a stretch.) Should he say that he prioritized Frank's work? That was silly, besides specious. Frank prioritized his own work. He smirked. Should he mention bringing coffee for everyone whenever there was a meeting in Frank's office? (That had happened more than once.) He admitted that the words, as written, made him sound more like a secretary than anything else, but what could he add? If Frank would only define his duties, he'd try to put the best face on it, of course, but now it felt like slathering paint on an imaginary canvas.

He looked at his typewriter, brought it forward to the center of his desk. Maybe he should just doodle? Make up words? And phrases. Like he'd done to stimulate himself when he was a poet. Would that give him the requisite inspiration? Put him in the mood?

He frowned and rolled a sheet of paper into the typewriter, feeling assertive at last. "Well, beef it up, Fairweather!" he admonished himself. "You wanted this job, so do it!"

In late May Frank, as promised, sent him to a course at the World Trade Center. Two hours, every Thursday afternoon for six weeks. Back in the classroom at last! Albeit as student, not teacher.

Rather to his surprise, Robert truly enjoyed his time there. First of all, he relished riding up to the sixtieth floor so quickly that his ears popped. Second, he found the instructor, a Mr. Oiseau who hailed from Chemical Bank, genial, on top of his subject, and obviously enjoying his own message.

The course was titled *Financing World Trade*, and each point was a genuine revelation for Robert. He'd never once considered how sending things abroad, or receiving products from abroad, might involve financing. What opportunities exporting and importing creates for banks! How does the sender pay for such shipments? How does the receiver accept the shipment, and pay for getting it off the docks and into the right hands? Lines of credit! Selling open invoices to increase a seller's cash flow! Opportunities for protecting a business's credit risk! Enhancing balance sheet liquidity! Improving collection time! None of these were subjects he found inherently interesting but he'd always relished learning new things –- and just think! He might one day be able to contribute to this process, once he'd mastered this completely novel world! Each afternoon when he returned from the class, he felt buoyed. Stimulated. Even happy.

It was early August. He'd been working as Frank Gross's right-hand-man for six months when his boss beckoned him into his office. A lot had happened in that time, but very little to make to make Robert feel more comfortable in his new position. He was barely seated when Frank, betraying a certain excitement, said, "Bobby, first of all, I don't think I thanked you enough for the edits you made to my speech to the banking conference I attended a while back. I made a pretty big splash there."

Splash-splash, thought Robert, then mentally pinched himself.

"And that's partly thanks to you. So, good job and thank you for that."

"You're welcome, Frank. I . . ."

"But what I'm excited about now is"—he continued— "I think I've found a project that you can really get your teeth into, and I expect you to knock it out of the park."

Well! That sounded good! Robert leaned forward in his chair, a quizzical smile hovering, waiting to bloom. "Gee, thanks, Frank, that's nice of you—"

"Bobby, what do you know about Zero Based Budgeting?"

Should he try a quip? "Zero?"

A moment's hesitation, then, "Which may give me a leg up, right? Actually, the only thing I know now is that it's what President Carter is proposing the federal government do for the next fiscal year. I know that only thanks to the *New York Times*."

"Spot on. And if the feds can do it, we can too. Not only am I in favor of it, a proponent, so to speak, but I've just got word from upstairs that *we're* planning to do it. CMFB will do Zero Based Budgeting for our next fiscal year, which starts in September. So here's the deal: I need someone to explain it to everyone and teach them how to do it. I think you're the man for the job. I want to make you my explainer-in-chief for ZBB!"

"Oh! Well, that certainly sounds interesting. And I rather think I'd enjoy that kind of assignment, Frank. First, I'll need to study it a little bit of course, so I'd feel comfortable explaining it to others."

"Stands to reason! But the theory behind it is actually quite simple. What it means is that . . . well, let me put it like this. The way businesses have done budgeting in the past, the way it's pretty much always been done is, you look at what your budget was for last year and you add on. That means everything that's in your budget, of course—personnel, supplies, space, the whole ball of wax."

He paused to take a breath.

"Which pretty much means that you're spending more next year than last. In fact, almost always. But is that really what you want to do, given your goals? The difference with ZBB is that you start each year, each time you're building your budget for the following year, at ground zero. You start from scratch. Forget last year's budget. What are you expecting to accomplish going forward? And how many people will you need to accomplish it, as well as how much of everything else—supplies, equipment, etc."

"I can see that." said Robert. "So I'm guessing you could describe it as a method of budgeting in which all expenses must be justified and approved for each new period."

"You got it. I have some stuff you can read but I agree with the men upstairs that it makes a lot of sense, and I'd like you to help me out on this. You're the point man. I'd like you to be my explainer-in-chief to all the different units under my command as they begin their contemplation of what they're asking for upstairs in next year's budget."

"And when might that start?"

"Sometime in the next couple of weeks. So read up, think what your approach is gonna be and when you're primed, you'll schedule yourself to meet with all my managers. And so, you'll talk 'em through it. I'll give you a list of who's who on Monday. Sound good?"

A pleased look came over Robert's face. "Sounds fine, Frank. Looking forward to it. I assume there'll be a memo going out to all these people before I begin inserting myself into their lives?"

"Of course, Bobby. It'll go out before the end of the week."

Robert swept out of the office in a pleasantly thoughtful frame of mind. Well, isn't this is a nice development? A substantive challenge! The assignment certainly boosted his importance a bit. Made him feel valued. At last, something he could get his teeth into! Explainer-in-chief. I can do that.

So when Frank plopped his returned Personnel forms on Robert's desk later that week (they'd asked for a third re-submission), our hero's first thought was, "Aha! No problem! Now I can include the ZBB assignment! That should certainly convince them of my usefulness."

ZBB, Robert discovered, was a bit more taxing, or at least more formalized, than what Frank had explained to him off the cuff that first day. What needed to happen was that the lowest-level manager was asked to develop what was called a *Decision Unit Determination*, meaning he compiled a budget for his office from scratch. Or he might even do three: a zero-funding level, a current funding level, and an enhanced service level. Once done, his particular *Decision Unit*, like all the others, was passed up to his supervisor, who, after examining all *Decision Units* under his control, assembled a *Decision Package* out of all his units, after eliminating (or revising) what he thought was unnecessary or undesirable to accomplish his goals. Whereupon—Robert imagined a big drum roll in the background as this happened—the top brass performed a "Ranking" of said packages. Which was most important? Which less, and so on. That's what the CEO would see in order to make his final determination.

Robert spent a good deal of time brainstorming about those elements and dreaming up ways of explaining each of them so as, he thought to make it all easier and more comprehensible. Charts? Graphs? Slides? Similes?

However. A couple of weeks later, it wasn't working out the way he'd supposed. His actual experience explaining

ZBB turned out to be not only disappointing but deflating. He'd done the necessary homework, boned up on the concept, and had felt fully prepared when he had his first meeting with managers. Some in that gathering had tried to be respectful, but there was a sullenness, a felt edge of resentment even from those who didn't speak up. And as the meetings continued, it dawned on him that they all viewed ZBB one way: as an effort to get rid of people. He came to realize that the most expensive element of most budgets was personnel. Clearly, they feared being fired. An attempt to convince them of the overall value *to the company* did little good. The whole process, in fact, made them feel vulnerable. And the lower the level of those who were being asked to consider afresh what choices they should make, the stronger the resistance.

He tried humor. He tried humility. He tried being responsive to their fears, assuring them that it was by no means an attempt to get rid of anybody, just an effort to create a more sensible approach to achieving their common goals.

But it didn't work. And, of course, the fact that he— Robert— was the face of ZBB for the corporation only added to the resistance. Who was this just-hired upstart with no background in finance or experience in the banking world who was telling them what to do? Robert continually tried to adjust his approach to see if he could mollify their fears, but nothing worked. They drew into themselves, became even more leaden. He might as well have been talking into a vacuum.

When he reported this back to Frank, he was told to ignore it and press on. It was company policy; it had to be done.

There was one exception. The head of computer programming, a very friendly nerd named Donald Prendergast, was totally receptive. Donald was a small, wiry, forty-year-old leprechaun with a quick wit and a surprising jamboree of freckles across the bridge of his nose who was immediately enthusiastic. A month or so earlier Robert had caught a ride with Donald up to Westchester when Frank—celebrating that now he was a bona-fide Senior Vice President—held a party for every one of those in his expanded squad at his recently acquired and rather magisterial estate. Donald had cracked jokes and talked freely with him and the two other passengers in his car, who happened to be Willy Loo and Peter Kleindienst, Robert's erstwhile lunch buddies. It was a gathering where Frank had even asked Robert to perform a bit—to read a few of his poems as part of the evening's entertainment. (Showing off his new protégé? Robert wondered.) The poems, though, however dramatically delivered, had fallen to the floor like dust motes and disappeared into the deep pile carpeting. To be sure, Frank's wife had liked them, as she had assured him in the kitchen while the party was breaking up.

But what was newly positive about Donald's reception

to ZBB training became clear early on in Robert's presentation to that group. Donald *wanted* to replace his entire unit, especially the out-of-date computers he'd been saddled with. "Citibank is eating us alive," he'd complained. "They are so far ahead of us in computing power and sophistication that it's pathetic. We need to get rid of every machine in my shop and get better stuff. The good stuff. The really good stuff." So Donald had been happy with the notion of going back to zero and staring over. And, clearly, the approach he favored would include *more* personnel, not less.

With that one exception, Robert came to consider his efforts—regrettably—a dismal failure.

And somehow, the grass roots resistance (or something else mysterious and ineffable?) bore fruit. The policy was suddenly reversed—the Seventeenth Floor changed its mind. Word came down, Frank bit the bullet, Robert's place in the sun suffered an eclipse, and everyone went back to budgeting the same way.

Less than a week later, Robert's chair disappeared. *How dare they!* he thought, and when evening fell, he immediately began scouring the conference rooms, finally spotting it; he was sure it was the one. He grabbed it and wheeled it out into the hallway —where he drew up short before an impressive looking gentleman in a Brooks Brothers suit. The man stood in the broad hallway, smiling softly at Robert, one hand supporting his chin while the other cupped an elbow.

"Midnight requisition, is it?" the man said.

"Well, yes. Someone stole my chair. I needed to get it back."

"You're Frank's Executive Assistant, are you not? Is that your title? Pleased to meet you. I'm Michael Knickerbocker."

He'd heard the name, he was sure. Not in Frank's wheelhouse. But like Frank, Robert was convinced, an SVP.

"The pleasure is mine, Mr. Knickerbocker. Yes, I'm Robert Fairweather."

"Quite. Let me ask you something, Robert. You do realize, do you not, that there's no such thing as *Executive Assistant*? To a Senior Vice President?"

"Beg pardon?"

"The title. That title does not exist. Three years ago, I believe, it was abolished. Wiped out. No one has an Executive Assistant. Nowhere in CMFB."

"I'm sorry?"

"I'll bet you are. And I'm sorry to be the bearer of bad news. But your position, I'm afraid, is simply imaginary. A chimera. Have a good evening, Mr. Fairweather. Enjoy your chair."

And off he walked in the opposite direction from Frank's office. Robert stood in the hallway for a full minute, heart beating loudly in his chest, before turning to wheel his precious cargo back to his office.

And the very next day, the hammer came down hard. Activity there was, but of a frenetic variety, nothing that seemed deliberate and purposeful. Some wandered the halls looking dazed, cut loose from their moorings. At noon a distraught Frank swept into the cubicle outside his office. Robert stared at him, wondering what was going on.

"Bobby, here's your new assignment," he said, handing him a single sheet of paper, apparently a directive from the Personnel Office. "You're to report to Hal McCloskey on the third floor sometime today. He'll tell you what you're supposed to do." With that, he strode into his office.

Robert was stunned, not to mention perplexed. He took a minute, then rose and entered Frank's office, found him staring out the window.

"I don't understand, Frank. What's happening? What's going on to cause all this . . . upheaval?"

Frank smiled, but not a happy smile. More like one might see on a clown at the Big Apple Circus.

"They're not my troops anymore, Bobby. My office is being disbanded. It's going back to the way it used to be."

"And what about your job?"

"My job? Oh, they won't fire me. At least I don't think so. And I seriously doubt they'll demote me. But they'll find another position. Somewhere. Right now, I'm still in the dark. But you're no longer my assistant and that paper I gave you shows who you report to. Any time you get your stuff ready, you're to go down. As you can see, it's on the 3rd Floor. Now leave me, please. I need to think."

And that was the last time he saw Frank Gross. Staring out the window at a world that had turned upside down.

Robert gathered all the personal papers on or in his desk, stuffed them into his briefcase, and looked around. Should he take his chair? he thought absurdly. His treasured midnight requisition? He left his office (was it ever his office?) and walked down the hallway, chairless, toward the elevator.

Robert finished out his last month at CMFB under Mr. McCloskey, working an adding machine. He appeared to be a staff [?] of one. There were several desks, but no other people. McCloskey was not an unfriendly sort, but it was clear he was skeptical of Robert's fitness for the tasks assigned. It appeared to Robert that his new boss thought he'd been sent a useless intellectual type (he must have heard something, Robert supposed, of his background) who didn't know his ass from his elbow when it came to numbers. But Robert doggedly pursued the copying and adding of digits as he was asked to, hour after hour—not fast, but tenaciously. He was told from the outset he'd be kept on the payroll for one month only, until the reorganization was complete, then let go and eligible for unemployment.

So a month after he'd descended to the third floor, as certain as that Christmas comes but once a year, as sure as there's a summer solstice and an autumnal equinox, he left CMFB for good. As he rode the elevator down and passed through the revolving glass doors for the last time, he wasn't sure what he was feeling.

In the courtyard, he stared a moment at the sculpture: the squiggly worm of toothpaste that was every passerby's introduction to CMFB. As he did so, there popped into his mind what a graph of his banking career might look like. Perhaps a sharply rising line ascending to an apex where it would drop ever more steeply down. To nil. To zero. And way below those two lines would be a third, totally flat, representing his salary, which had never changed. He'd spent almost two years at US Customs & Marketing Federal Bank, promised the moon—a sterling and lucrative career—yet had only been paid as a printer.

Oh, well, he thought, as he moved toward the nearest subway. Another learning curve.

THE DECISION

Robert Fairweather sat at his chessboard, study-ing the pieces with laser-like intensity. A book lay open on the coffee table, listing famous games of masters through the ages. Robert had only recently learned chess, from a friend at the bank where he'd worked—a Rumanian in his fifties named Alexandru Balan, who claimed that one of his winning games had been featured in *The New York Times*—and Robert had by now discovered how much he relished the total absorption this pastime required. It was, in fact, the only satisfactory way he'd found to fruitfully pass hour after hour without spending a dime.

The game he was focused on at the moment was a "Ruy Lopez" played by Emanuel Lasker and J. R. Capablanca in St. Petersburg in 1914, , one which the great Capablanca was slated to lose. Lasker, playing white, had just made his latest move, his 35th, which the book's author had marked with an exclamation point, since it was the unexpected, even startling move by white that led to Capablanca's downfall. Robert was trying to puzzle out why Capablanca's 34th move was such a serious error.

The phone rang, and Robert jumped.

Who the fuck could that be? he wondered, his petulance sparked by the fact that a) it was ten o'clock at night and—this being a Thursday—he had to work the next day, and b) he almost never received phone calls these days, since his social life seemed to be a thing of the remote past.

He thought at first to let it ring and find out later whether the caller had left a message. But he'd lost his concentration anyway, so after the third ring, he sighed, deserted the board game for a perch closer to the phone, and picked up.

"Yes?" he said gruffly.

"Hello," a sweet female voice answered. "Is this Dr. Fairweather?"

Doctor Fairweather? Nobody called him Dr. Fairweather these days.

"It is," he answered. "Who's calling, please?"

"Robert, this is Nicoletta Kagin. I'm a professor at Hollins College in Virginia."

He shook his head in disbelief. Found himself silently laughing.

"Ah, well. Nicoletta, I know who *you* are. From where I sit right at this moment, I can see the three-volume collection of Russian philosophy which you edited, prominently displayed in my living room library. However, what I can't imagine is how you happen to know *my* name!"

"Ah. Let me tell you first why I called. Then I'll fill you in on how I came by your name. I'm calling, Robert, because I'm chairing a session for the American Association for the Advancement of Slavic Studies, which is taking place in Atlanta this year, in December. It's a session on Russian philosophy and I'd like to ask you to present a paper on Nicholas Berdiaev.

"As to the other matter, someone who had recently returned from the Soviet Union spoke to someone over there who knew you."

Excuse me? thought Robert. *I'm known in the Soviet Union and virtually anonymous in the United States! Go figure! Wait! Could that visitor, whoever he or she might have been, have spoken to Masha Ospensko?* Which prompted another name entering his head.

"George Quinn!" he burst out.

"You got it, Robert," said Nicoletta. "Good guess. He also read a paper of yours, I believe, based on your dissertation."

"But that paper was never published! The *Slavic Review* turned it down!"

"I know. A five-man committee. It was a 2-3 vote. George was one of the two votes who wanted to publish it."

"Hah! Well, how about that! I never knew. It's a pretty small world after all."

"Certainly in our field it is, Robert. Now, to my question. Would you be interested in writing a paper for the convention?"

Robert was quiet a moment. The irony of the situation had seized him like a vise. He didn't know whether to laugh or cry.

"Nicoletta," he said slowly, "I'm flattered you're asking me, really I am. So honored. But I'm afraid I can't. Number one, I'm no longer affiliated with any university. I no longer have a teaching job, Nicoletta. For several years now. I'm typing for a living. I'm basically broke. In fact, I have to go to bed soon so I may rise early and catch the subway to my typing job. There's no way I could possibly find the time to put together a paper on Berdiaev. Nor could I afford the plane flight down to Atlanta. In fact, I'd be hard-pressed to cough up enough money for the registration fee!"

He paused a moment, embarrassed. He'd realized his voice was becoming too raw, too strident. "So, I'm sorry. Thank you so very much for asking. It was incredibly nice of you to think of me. But I'm afraid it's just not possible."

After a brief pause, she said, "What about your paper? The one that got turned down by the *Slavic Review*?"

He laughed softly. "It's thirty-six pages long, Nicoletta. In fact, that may have been one of their reasons for rejecting it. How long are these convention papers supposed to be?"

"Twenty minutes, that's the limit. But couldn't you shorten it? Boil it down a bit? Pick out the main points?"

Robert sighed. "I don't see how. From thirty-six pages to . . . what? Ten? Eight? No, I'm afraid I couldn't do it. I have neither the time nor the money. So, unfortunately, the answer is no."

She was silent for a few beats. Then, "Well, Robert, I'm sorry to hear it. I really think it could be a fitting contribution. Listen, why don't you think about it? Maybe there's a way. Think about it, okay? Promise me that. Just tell me you'll think about it."

Robert wondered if there was supposed to be some kind of magic in saying those three words three times? Should you also twirl and clap your hands? Abracadabra! Success!

"I'm not likely to change my mind, Nicoletta. My circumstances are what they are. But I will think about it. And thank you again."

"Good, Robert. Very glad to hear it. I'll call you soon."

Two or so weeks later, this time on a Friday, the phone rang again. It was a little earlier in the evening than before; he was not playing, plotting, or analyzing chess but washing the one plate, one bowl and one spoon he'd dirtied with his evening meal. It was a good meal, he thought: chili. He made a damned fine chili, in his opinion and, as always, he'd made enough to last him across multiple days. Today was the end of the line, however, so he'd also need to wash the pot. He dried his hands and went to the phone.

He entertained a faint hope it might be the pretty young

woman who'd checked out his groceries at the supermarket three days ago, when he'd purchased the makings for the chili. Ink-black hair, dark eyes, full lips, a nice laugh. He'd mentioned in passing that he played chess and she'd looked impressed. Perhaps this was her begging to come over and play? But he was pretty certain he knew who it was.

Once his suspicions had been confirmed, he said, "Nice to speak to you again, Nicoletta. Thanks for calling. But I'm afraid I haven't changed my mind about the paper. Still can't see my way clear to managing it. Still broke, and not a rich uncle in sight. So, much as I'd enjoy the opportunity to talk about my favorite Russian philosopher, I really can't see the point."

"There's still time, you know. It's a month and a half away yet. Ample time to revise your presentation."

"But even if I could afford it, what would be the point, Nicoletta? For me, I mean? Would I expect someone who hears it to suddenly offer me a position? Putting aside not having the money to travel. Or even the 35 bucks to register."

A brief pause, then she began again.

"Actually, Robert, a convention is a good place, *a very good place*, to make contacts, so you never know, there may well be positions opening up that would be first heard about there. Hey, if I were a top university in the process of recruiting someone for a position in Russian or Slavic history, I'd certainly make a point of showing up. I'd say it's even likely."

He sighed and rolled his eyes, happily aware, of course, that she couldn't see. Before he could work out a satisfactory reply, however, she continued.

"And as far as the money is concerned, let me put it this way. I don't know what the plane fare is from New York to Atlanta, but night flights, I expect, especially with one of the no-frills airlines that are operating these days, are pretty cheap. And I'm sure you could find reasonable accommodations a decent distance from the convention center. Keep in mind, you wouldn't have to stay at the posh hotel set aside for the convention, which I've no doubt is costing people an arm and a leg, and that they're paying for out of some department's slush fund. And as far as the registration fee is concerned: Goodness gracious! Why pay it? I'm familiar with the hotel where it's being held, so I can tell you which side door to enter, how to pass through the halls undetected and show up at the room your event is scheduled in—without ever signing in or getting a nametag! In fact, I could mail you a nametag in advance. So that's one hurdle eliminated."

Through all this Robert could not help smiling and shaking his head. Boy, she was good! he thought. Is there no objection I could make she wouldn't have an answer for? How on earth had she been seized by Russian studies, anyway? She could have been a courtroom lawyer!

"Nicoletta, I thank you for the extra thought you've put into this, for trying your darnedest to make it easier for me, but I still have to say, 'I don't think so.' I just can't see my way clear to finding the time that would be required to write a new twenty-minute paper. I don't believe I could take sufficient time away from my job to get it done without impoverishing myself even more. You're very persuasive, but I'm afraid my answer is still no."

"Well, think about it," she said. "Give it just a bit more thought. I'd love to see you there, Robert. I'll call you one more time, in just one week. Okay?"

He smiled. How could he say no to that? "Okay," he said. "I don't expect to change my mind, but I promise you I'll give it some serious thought."

"What more can I ask? Good to speak to you, Robert. Talk to you later. Goodbye."

After he hung up, he did not immediately move. He sat and pondered for a long while. He wasn't thinking about the girl with the ink-black hair and the charming laugh. He wasn't thinking about chess. Nor was he thinking about the invitation that his friend Mortimer had extended him to come up to his (their) old (Columbia) neighborhood tomorrow night and have a few beers at their favorite haunts, perhaps trundle down the stairs at Orsini's, the bar where Robert had once worked in his graduate school days and sing a few songs around Angelo Orsini's piano. He wasn't thinking about any of those things.

Eventually, he rose and walked, several times, around

his apartment. Circling around the bed, first on one side, then on the other. Into the bathroom and out again. Around the living room, circling, again and again, as a hawk might, before moving through the kitchen into the hallway and heading for the bedroom once more.

After a good while, he searched his files and found the paper he had written years ago for the *Slavic Review*. He retreated to the kitchen table and began to read. After scanning four or five pages he tossed the article aside and pushed back his chair. Yet he continued to sit, thinking. What he was ruminating about, all this while, was Berdiaev, that strange, brilliant, contradictory philosopher whom he'd studied for so long, who was both deeply mystical and fiercely political. Finally, around midnight, he rose, filled the vessel he'd used for his chili with warm water, left it on the stove to soak, and went to bed.

The next morning, he rose early. After making fresh coffee, washing last night's pot, pouring himself a bowl of Kellogg's raisin bran and milk, he found the article he'd tossed aside the previous evening, began to read it again. By the time he'd read five pages and finished his cereal, he pushed the bowl back , tossed the article aside once more, reached for his typewriter and began to write.

The first thing he wrote down was a title, which his mind had cooked up in bed the previous evening, just before he fell asleep. Not the same paper or a condensation, he'd told himself then. Same subject, new approach.

Then he wrote for five hours straight, the words tumbling out, consulting no notes, reading nothing more, just writing. He checked no sources, though he made parenthetical notations where he intended to insert a quote he was certain would illustrate his point. Some quotes he almost knew by heart anyway.

After slapping together a cheese sandwich for lunch, he munched while still pecking away at the typewriter.

Around four in the afternoon, he finally stopped, shook his head to clear it and drew a slow, deep breath. Then he began searching in his old, thirty-six-page paper the quotes he was planning to insert. Once located, using typewriter, scissors and scotch tape, he slotted them in at the appropriate place. When he'd finished this task, he chuckled to himself, but lost no time in retyping his new paper, making corrections and improvements as he went.

By eleven o'clock that evening, he was finished. He set it aside. He'd polish it tomorrow. He was certain it would take no more than twenty minutes to read. Exhausted but happy, he went to bed.

Sunday, as planned, was devoted to polishing. Then reading for time. Which told him he needed to shorten one long quote and hack a few words from a couple of paragraphs. He was pleased that he'd still managed to make and consume three small meals during the day.

Monday, he called in sick and began the second part of his plan. First, after a little research, he found a booking at a hotel in Atlanta for one night, less than a mile from convention headquarters. An easy walk. Then he located the cheapest flight he could find and booked a late evening jaunt to Atlanta the evening before his paper was scheduled to be read. He still had a valid American Express Credit Card which, though a bit top-heavy, wasn't maxed out, and used that to pre-pay both the flight and the room. Next, he called Neil Sobieski, a friend and fellow historian from Brooklyn Quintessential University, his old workplace, who'd recently been promoted to Dean of Administration. It turned out that, yes, as a matter of fact, Neil did have a contact in Atlanta—someone he'd met a year ago at a national conference. Somewhat to Robert's surprise, he was happy, even eager, to do his fellow historian a favor. Robert then called Professor Antin in Georgia—Neil's contact—to see whether the fellow could meet him at the airport on the appropriate evening and ferry him to his chosen hotel? The answer was yes, of course, most assuredly, he'd be delighted, and would Robert have time to share a small meal with his family before?

At the end of the day, however risky it seemed to his finances—as had been the credit he'd placed on his American Express Card—Robert went forth to a local bar and had a drink. Just one. And all the way home he was smiling. The next time she called, he'd be ready.

❧

Robert sat at the speakers' table, hands folded above his paper, somewhat apprehensive, but marveling at the crowd. There must be 200 people in the audience! Chattering gaily, looking on expectantly. He was surprised, though quite pleased, that a session devoted to Russian philosophy should draw such a gathering. To his right at the table sat his fellow readers. All male. He knew none of them personally nor by reputation; both seemed a few years older than he. Nor had he made out what universities they represented. No doubt that information was inscribed on the nametags pinned to their suit lapels, but because they weren't in front of him, he couldn't read their tags. He supposed that information would be revealed when the fellow at the other end of the long table, who served both as chair and discussant, introduced them. It had already been determined that Robert was the third reader, to which he had no objections. Being last—the closer!—was a great position, was it not? His own convention nametag, sent him through the mail by Nicoletta, while identifying him as Dr. Robert Fairweather, specified no institution. And she, the one who invited him here—he found this strange— was nowhere to be seen.

The crowd was restive; people were still arriving. He fell to musing.

Getting here had turned out to be mostly free of pitfalls. The two-and-one-half hour flight was uneventful; he'd even managed to sleep for half an hour. Professor Antin, a middle-aged English professor specializing in Joyce, had a shiny bald pate except for a carefully tended patch around the ears. He'd picked Robert up at the airport and whisked him off to his home. There he'd eaten a late dinner with the professor and Mrs. Antin, a tall, angular lady with sparkling blue eyes, who had proved to be as pleasant and chatty as her husband. They'd commiserated appropriately over his difficult situation in New York and wished him all the luck in the world at the conference and on his return. Coffee and a scrumptious home-made apple pie had rounded out the meal, after which it had taken Antin a mere fifteen minutes to drop Robert at his no-frills hotel, where he'd gone to sleep within the hour and awakened in plenty of time to have a light breakfast before the 30-minute walk to the conference hotel.

Robert located the main entrance—knew to avoid it—and circled the hotel until he found a side door. Was it the right side door? Closest to the corner, wasn't that what Nicoletta had said? But which corner? Was there another side door at the other corner? He began to walk further, but after he'd gone ten steps, he changed his mind and returned to the first door. Once inside, the question became: which was the right room? He hadn't been given a room number, nor a schedule, but had assumed there would be signage announcing which room was set aside for which session. He glanced at his watch. Ten minutes. Plenty of time. He walked down the hall to the right, found an intersecting hall and decided to try that. So far, he'd seen only closed doors with no signage. He turned right into still another hallway. Was he now going the same way as he'd gone before? When he first entered? He stopped a moment. Was this a maze he was in? Perhaps he was really inside one of those English gardens with ten-foot-high hedges that lead you around and around to nowhere, looking for an exit. Why were there no signs? Why no open doors?

Suddenly he noticed a couple of older gentlemen standing outside an open doorway speaking Russian. He sighed with relief. What else could it be? But wait! This whole convention was devoted to Slavic subjects of one kind or another, wasn't it? He hesitated but decided to go in anyway and made his way to the front of the room until he'd found a table with placards with names on them. One of them his. Breathing a sigh of relief, he nodded to the other speakers, took his seat, opened his briefcase and extracted his paper.

Suddenly a hush fell over the audience when the man on his far right at the table rose to speak. He introduced himself and the panel, including Robert. Then he introduced the first speaker. And after him, the second. In each case, Robert barely attended to the content of their papers, trying to remain focused on what he was about to say.

Inevitably, though it still astonished him, it became his turn. As he listened to his own introduction, he found his outlook alternating, inadvertently, between that of the captain of a schooner navigating some tricky shoals and that of a prisoner just remanded into custody. This was a new experience. He'd taught many a class; had even, on invitation, spoken at one or two public meetings about subjects he was familiar with. And he'd attended a number of national conventions over the years—of the American Historical Association and of this one, the AAASS. But he'd never spoken at one. Never been personally asked to deliver a paper by a well-known colleague in his field. Nonetheless, when the chairperson took his seat and the moment arrived for Robert to stand and read, his apprehension melted away, in its place only the pleasant *frisson* he felt before any performance.

Robert was essentially making an argument. His subject was Berdiaev's relation to the Russian Revolution of 1905-1907—the same as the paper he'd earlier submitted to the *Slavic Review*. But what he'd done was to re-think it entirely, concentrating on four definable themes: socialism, anarchism, liberalism, and democracy. He'd titled the essay "Mysticism and Politics." Did Berdiaev—clearly a mystical philosopher by that time—embrace any of those political movements or ideas? The answer he'd ferreted out was both yes and no to each. And he'd marshaled citations to back up his thesis. He'd written in a brisk, breezy manner with, hopefully, just enough Russian words and phrases thrown in to clearly establish his familiarity with the subject. By the end he felt certain he'd held his audience captive. The applause was rewarding.

There was a long reception line and Robert, shaking hands and thanking each person for coming, was thrilled by the congratulations he was receiving. Suddenly, standing before him, number ten or eleven in the line, was a familiar face. A student of his that he'd not seen in ten years. Richard Applegate!

"O mi God! Richard! What a delightful surprise! How the hell are you? What brings you here? Are you teaching now?"

"Sure am, Dr. Fairweather! I'm an Assistant Professor at the University of Idaho. Russian history, just like I planned. And plenty of skiing to go with it."

Robert's first appointment had been at a small liberal arts college on the West Coast, and Richard had been a student in his very first Russian History class.

"God, how time flies! My earliest Russian History student now teaching Russian History! Passing it along! What a wonderful tribute! Will you be staying long enough for us to have a proper chat at some point?"

Although he did feel it as an homage, the irony did not escape Richard that his first student now had a teaching job, and *he* did not.

"Actually, I'm leaving on an afternoon flight in a couple of hours. So glad I could be around for your paper, though. It was smashing."

"Yeah, well, I'm on a night flight back to the Apple this

evening so I guess we'll have to communicate by letter, now that I know where you are. So good seeing you, Richard!"

They hugged again and the line moved on.

Now past noon, just as he'd begun thinking Nicoletta's phone calls had been a species of auditory hocus-pocus, she suddenly appeared. Greeting him warmly, she apologized for her absence (a visit to her cardiologist, but nothing to worry about) and told him she'd already heard a number of comments on how wonderfully his paper had been received. Made her feel proud to have been so persistent. A small woman in a fire-engine red frock with a full head of shocking white hair, her demeanor struck him, despite her scholarly accomplishments, as more akin to that of a chatty favorite aunt. He found her delightful.

"Would you like to meet Aaron Skolnick?"

Over lunch in the hotel dining room (her tab), she introduced him to the editor of the *Slavic Review*. Also at the table was a dour young fellow named Sergei Lopatin who was writing a dissertation hoping to prove that the Russian state had actually been formed a hundred years before the accepted version set forth in the Lavrentian chronicles. Professor Skolnick, he of the thick glasses and sparse, combed-back hair, was delighted to meet Robert, and—once Nicoletta had apprised him of Robert's situation—he revealed that *indeed* he knew of a position in Russian history for the following year that had just become available at Cornell University, and might Robert be interested in that? Its recruiter, a Dr. Mitchell Farnsworth, had needed to depart after the morning session but had told Professor Skolnick he should be certain to ask anyone he thought a suitable candidate to contact him directly at the Cornell History Department in Ithaca.

Robert could hardly believe his good fortune. He grinned at Nicoletta. It seems she'd been right after all!

A few weeks later, on a crisp, sunny January morning in 1977 Robert found himself walking toward an East Side hotel in the twenties. Two days earlier President Jimmy Carter had been inaugurated, and Robert had declared that to be a hopeful sign. His interview with Professor Showalter from Cornell was scheduled for 11:30. He felt nervous but also rather buoyant. He discovered the address to be a chic-looking, six-story building of a type sometimes referred to as a "boutique hotel." He checked his watch. Ten minutes early. Perfect.

When he knocked on the door a few minutes later he was admitted immediately. If there had been earlier candidates, no sign of them now.

Once they'd introduced themselves, Robert decided that Professor Showalter reminded him of Raymond Whitehall, his mentor at UCLA where he'd received his Master's. Showalter had the same easy affability, the same offhand, quiet presence as Dr. Whitehall and, in fact—with his ruddy complexion and thinning red hair—might almost have been mistaken for his twin.

Robert had enjoyed Whitehall's tutelage and guidance during those two years (now almost two decades gone), though he'd struck him as someone who'd been irretrievably wounded over the years, ground down by a system he found himself trapped within. In an unusually candid moment in his office, Whitehall had confided to Robert that when the university first hired him, they'd assured him that there were several ways, besides publishing another book (his dissertation had been brought out by a scholarly press), that one might fulfill the qualifications for promotion to Full Professor: serving on university-wide committees, for example. And Professor Whitehall, who didn't enjoy writing, had dutifully accepted every committee assignment that came his way over his two-decade career. But he told Robert, five years ago they'd reversed themselves—declaring publication to be the only criterion for advancement—and Whitehall now had to live with the fact that he would never be promoted to Full Professor.

Something in Showalter's demeanor triggered that memory: of a gracious, agreeable man somewhat worn down by bureaucracy and time.

Once they'd introduced themselves, Robert cast his eyes around the small room, with its two twin beds and only one armchair, and asked "Where should I sit?"

"Oh, the chair! Take the chair, please. I'll just perch

here on the edge of the bed, beside my briefcase. Sorry for the Spartan conditions. I realize it's not the Waldorf."

"No problem. Never been inside the Waldorf anyway. Have you been interviewing many candidates?"

"I suppose. Yes. Seven already, plus two in Atlanta and a couple in Chicago last week. You, in fact, are my last. I fly back to Ithaca later this afternoon."

"I imagine you'll be glad. Beautiful campus, Cornell. I was there once . I know someone who teaches Anthropology there. I visited him a few years back and was astonished at how beautiful it was."

"Can't think of another campus that tops it. I love living there. Well, Robert, you obviously have very strong credentials. Shall we get right to it?"

"Of course. Ask away."

The interview lasted a scant forty minutes. Robert felt perfectly at ease throughout, enjoyed talking about his experiences, his interests, his hopes. Rather like sharing a cup of coffee with a friend, he thought, though that immediately made him long for a cup.

When Showalter brought it to a close, they both rose and shook hands warmly.

"Oh, say," said Robert then. "Before I go, any way you can let me know what my chances are?"

"Afraid not, Dr. Fairweather. You're obviously a very strong candidate, which you must know, but I'm not allowed to reveal anything else. Making comparisons is just not kosher. And of course, I won't even be making the final decision. The whole department has to agree."

"I understand," said Robert. "I do." He turned away, then turned back. "However, . . . My circumstances are rather special, don't you think? I've been hoping to return to a respectable academic position for four years now, and I'd really like to know whether I'm fooling myself."

Showalter looked down and sighed. "I appreciate that," he said. "I do. You're clearly a very strong candidate. But, beyond that . . . the rules of the game are that I'm not allowed to tip my hand one way or the other. Sorry."

Robert sighed and looked away. Suddenly he remembered: How many times had Nicoletta asked him to be on her panel? Three, wasn't it? Was that a magic number? Or would he blow his chances completely by duplicating her persistence? He decided to take a chance.

"I wouldn't want to put you on the spot, Professor Showalter. Clearly, I'm not asking for a final verdict. But it's really important to me at this juncture to get a feel for my chances."

Showalter's turn to sigh. He looked out the window. Through a diaphanous white curtain, the clear January light shone brightly through.

"Well," he said. "I guess I can tell you this much, though I'd hope you wouldn't share it around. As I said, you strike a lot of the right notes. There's also another candidate—a woman—whose qualifications are, I would say, about the same strength. Now, Cornell University's history department, though quite wonderful, consists of 23 men and one woman. In the current environment, you know, a few years after Title IX and all that, we feel under a lot of pressure . . . well, I guess you can see where this might be going. That's all I can say."

Robert nodded, extended his hand again and they shook. "Thank you, Dr. Showalter. I appreciate your candor. It means a lot to me. Have a wonderful day and a safe trip home."

On the short ride down in the elevator he felt withdrawn, but once he got outside and began walking through the beautiful, luminous weather, his mood lightened. He allowed himself a faint smile.

"That's it, then," he said to himself, and took a deep breath. "Now I know. I'm not sorry I wrote that paper. But that was my last hurrah."

PRESSURE POINTS

Robert awoke to darkness and a clamorous noise along Myrtle Avenue.

He'd returned home that afternoon from his job at the bank, wolfed down a quick dinner from leftovers scrounged from his fridge and, still sleep-deprived from an erratic rest the night before, passed out on his living room daybed. Startled awake now, he was perplexed, certain the living room light had been on when he'd lay down. And the air conditioning. Why had it become so warm? He noticed the luminous dial of his wristwatch said 9:45 PM. Quickly he rose and scrambled over to his large picture windows, nearly tripping over a leg of his coffee table.

Outside was dark, as well. And no doubt hot, it being the middle of July. But from his twelfth-floor perch he discerned vague small shapes moving quickly. Was that a flood of marauding insects swarming along Myrtle Ave? Then came the sound of breaking glass. Frowning, he slid open one window; the hubbub swelled to a roar. The avenue was scarcely half a football field away, and he realized suddenly that those dark, moving shapes were people—running, shouting, scrambling along the sidewalk. Another burst of breaking glass.

Out of nowhere suddenly came police cars, sirens screaming, headlights and spotlights illuminating people as they dashed along sidewalks and streets, laden with objects. Sometimes big things: he could make out two figures loping uncertainly while lugging something heavy between them. Then, one after another, brakes squealed and cops tumbled, batons raised, out of their cars, chasing the looters. The beams from their vehicles cast the marauding figures in a bizarre light.

He glanced toward the Manhattan Bridge, normally visible from this window. Not now. He cast his eyes again around his living room. No light anywhere. His gaze swept outward once more, past the invisible bridge. Nothing.

So that confirmed it: not only was Brooklyn in a blackout; so was the rest of the city.

At that moment, his phone rang. Robert was so startled that he jumped. "Who in the world . . . ?" he said aloud but made his way carefully in the dark toward the phone table. He picked up. "Hello?" he said.

"Hello, Robert! This is Jackie!"

"Jackie? Sorry, I don't . . ."

"Jackie Floyd, you shmuck! Your partner from the massage class. You mean you don't remember me?"

He was mortified.

"Oh, God! Jackie, I'm sorry. I didn't recognize . . . I mean, Jackie is also a man's name, but your voice is so clearly a woman's that . . . ."

"Be still a moment, willya? I want to invite you to come see me. Would you like to come over to my place in Manhattan? Soho? I can fix us some food if we need it. And I'm lonely; my roommate is elsewhere."

"Hey! Uh, well, what a wonderful idea, but . . . there's no subway running, I'm sure. I assume you're immersed in the blackout too, right?"

"Of course! We're all in the same boat. Which is why what I would really love is some company. Have you forgotten I have a car?"

"Hah! Well, I guess I had. Are you saying you'd come by to pick me up?"

"Of course, you silly! I can leave in five minutes, and I should be there in half an hour at the most. Downtown Brooklyn, right?"

"Uh, yes. You sure it's safe to travel, with the Blackout and all?"

"My car has headlights, dummy, and I'm absolutely sure there's not much traffic. So. Is it a date?"

"Well, gosh, yes! Of course! I'd love to see you, Jackie. So yes! Absolutely! I'll get ready to crawl down the twelve flights of my building to the lobby. Very carefully. And meet you in the parking lot. Are you sure you want to go to all this trouble? I mean, I can hardly believe my luck!"

"Well, give me the address, sport, and tell me how to get there. Let's get moving."

He gave her directions, emphasizing that she should take the Brooklyn rather than the Manhattan Bridge, so she could avoid passing Myrtle Avenue, still noisy with strife. Then he cradled the phone and smiled a silly smile. "Well, I'll be damned," he said softly to himself. "Jacqueline Floyd. What a lark!"

They had met, as she'd mentioned, in a massage class. Robert, who had tried many avenues during these lean times toward making additional money, had conceived of possibly learning massage and working up a small side business, offering his skills to whomever he could find as a client. Not during the day of course, when he'd be at work. But on evenings and weekends. He'd enjoyed a few relaxing and energizing Swedish massages himself in times past, but on each occasion had come away with the impression that, with a little training, he'd be capable of doing the same thing. Then he'd spotted a two-week course, offered in the evening, in both Shiatsu and Swedish massage, taught out of a Manhattan YWCA. The price was not prohibitive (if he put it on his credit card), and he figured, it might mean more earnings down the line, so why not? He'd enrolled.

The instructor was a somewhat chunky but muscular

woman in her late thirties, a Ms. Biederman, who had obviously studied both techniques quite thoroughly. She proved to be an excellent teacher. There was much to learn, but he found it fascinating, both the Swedish techniques as well as the Shiatsu, or acupressure. Within the Swedish component there were a myriad of strokes. There was effleurage, there was kneading, friction (rarely). There was the knife-edge motions of the hands. There was sawing, tendon rolling, pushing and pulling, the double-hand press, picking up, cupping with one hand while pressing and sliding with the other toward the cupped area. When to go deep, when to back off. No part of the body was neglected: back and neck, shoulders, the back of the legs and the buttocks. The heel, the instep, the sole. There was the head, the abdomen, the face, the arms, the chest. Using the fingers, using the palms, using the heel of the hand. There was friction and pounding (not too hard!), rolling. All these different modes were learned; each of them practiced repeatedly.

The shiatsu was equally fascinating, though Robert was skeptical at first. Perhaps because it was less traditional, he found it more difficult to locate, at the beginning, the "pressure points." But when he was able to identify the correct areas to apply thumb pressure (careful, not too much), he began to appreciate what the technique could accomplish to relieve tension in the body. Particularly did he feel that he'd eventually developed a skill with those locations in the shoulders as well as the three important pressure points at the base of the skull.

At the beginning of the first class, Ms. Biderman had everyone introduce themselves and explain their interest. She stressed that each attendee should wear loose, comfortable clothing, and then also said she needed everyone to choose a partner, so that they would have someone to practice on who would in turn practice on them.

Only a moment after that instruction was given, Jackie Floyd, a slim, good-looking, thirty-five-year-old brunette with enormous blue eyes who had identified herself during the requisite introductions as a modern dancer and dance teacher, had approached Robert and asked could she be his partner? He'd been more than happy to consent, and they'd remained partners throughout. He thought she was attractive (read: wonderful), and they seemed also to work beautifully with each other in class, each developing a sixth sense for where the other's tension resided, and, with growing confidence, applying the appropriate remedies to reduce it. He was smitten.

After the final class, he'd decided to ask her out. She'd consented, and they'd gone on a date at a restaurant on the Upper West Side (one of his old Columbia hangouts) in whose basement he knew they could later dance. It had been a wonderful date, and they'd seemed each to enjoy the other's company very much, loved dancing together, were amazed and delighted to discover that they'd both been born in Oklahoma ("how rare is that!" she'd exclaimed!), plus she was impressed to learn that he was an ex-college professor. *But*, as she explained to him on that occasion, she would soon be moving to the University of Southern Indiana to assume a position as the Deputy Director for Modern Dance, and a long-time boyfriend she'd met and lived with in Hawaii was coming to stay with her in Indiana to see whether they were ready to make it permanent, so starting up something with Robert didn't seem like a good idea, did it?

At the end of the evening, just before putting her on a city bus for her trip back to her apartment in Soho, he'd impulsively taken her in his arms, kissed her, and in almost an act of desperation, slipped his tongue past her lips and into her mouth. When they drew apart a moment later, she looked dazed, and stumbled onto the bus with seemingly a fond look back, but that was that. It had been perhaps two weeks from that night to this phone call.

Did it make any more sense now than it did then? he wondered. But, what the hell? It would be nice to see her again. Besides, it's a blackout, and she's picking me up in her car!

She was there in half an hour, in a Volkswagen beetle, and Robert was waiting, just inside the revolving doors of his building. He walked out and climbed into the car.

"Not a lot of leg room," he said, raising an eyebrow. "And here I was, expecting a Bentley."

"Don't knock my wonderful vehicle, wiseass," she said, "or I'll dump you somewhere on the Brooklyn Bridge. This steed has served me well for three years now. I call him Pinocchio. Been all across the country in it."

"Just kidding, youngster. Thank you so much for picking me up. This is really special of you. And so unexpected! Really! What a lovely surprise that you called."

"Nobody I'd rather share the total dark with." She laughed.

They were quiet awhile.

"So how you been in the two weeks since I last saw you?" he asked. "Anything changed?"

She glanced at him and returned her eyes to her driving. "Nothing much," she said finally. "And I'm fine. My roomy, Stephanie, left yesterday for Vermont, on vacation. She has family there. How about you?"

"Same old same old. Still trying to make my way as a banker. Which feels weird, I have to tell you."

"Any banking going on in Russia? I'd think they'd assign you there in a heartbeat, with your expertise and all."

"North America, South America, Middle East, Europe, and Asia," he recited, almost in a singsong. "Those are the international banking groups. We have no presence in the Soviet Union. And I wouldn't expect any."

"Seriously, with your dynamite background, a PhD and all—and now you've become a banker? What a waste! No plans to reapply to another university somewhere?"

A PhD and all. All what? He was glad she was impressed, of course, but what it unearthed from his memory was the bittersweet trifecta of 1971: in the same year he'd been awarded the degree, visited Russia for the first time, and been fired from his job. "Been six years now," he said. "That ship has sailed. At the moment I consider myself a poet. And I hope to do some other writing as well, perhaps, down the road."

They grew silent. It took very little time to reach her apartment. The streets leading to the Brooklyn Bridge, the bridge itself, the East Side Highway visible from their windows, the streets leading up through Wall Street and Chinatown to Soho, all utterly deserted. They saw only one other vehicle during the entire trip. A yellow cab. Seemingly empty. When she pulled up in front of her building, she found the same parking space she'd left a little more than an hour before.

They entered the building and climbed three flights to her apartment.

"I've made sandwiches," she said. "And I'll give you some quilts and pillows to take up to the roof and spread out for us. I'll be up with the goodies in a moment."

Thanks to the Blackout, the view from the roof was spectacular. For the first time since he'd been in New York City, Robert could see stars. And they flooded the sky. It reminded him most of summer nights on the ranch in California when he was a kid. Evenings he'd camped out in a sleeping bag on his lawn.

When Jackie pushed open the roof door and stepped out into the warm July evening, carrying her paper bag full of goodies, he noticed she'd changed from jeans into a light summer frock. Yellow. A good choice against her well-tanned skin. She looked lovely. She'd even managed to find a flower for her hair. When she lowered herself beside him, he realized she'd also dabbed on some perfume.

While they ate their sandwiches and chocolate chip cookies, Jackie announced that they could now watch a spectacular stage show, which she knew would happen at this hour. The building next door was one floor higher than hers and also had large picture windows, with drapes that had been pulled back. Candles had been lit, so there was some light in the rooms. And just as Jackie had whisperingly predicted, a woman soon appeared in the living room. Totally naked. Also, seriously corpulent.

"Now watch!" said Jackie. "She's going to move from that room to another, farther to the left and, for a moment, she'll entirely vanish. The room is just as lighted, it's apparently a passageway straight through, but she'll totally disappear. Then when she gets to a third room, she appears again! It's magic! I have no idea how to explain it. You watch!"

He did, and it unfolded just as she'd predicted. The woman then walked back the other way, and the same disappearing act happened again. Robert was amused but, though naked, the woman was so spectacularly obese that it was anything but titillating. He laughed along with Jackie—finding pleasure in the almost childish glee she took from her discovery—but truth to tell, his mind was on other things. When the show (to him, a sideshow) seemed officially over, he turned and looked a long time at her face, so clearly visible at this moment thanks to the spectacular show of stars above them, her large, sparkling blue eyes, the lips to which had recently been applied a crimson gloss.

On they talked, she in her kibitzing, somewhat smart-alecky voice, he with his more sober and occasionally sardonic one. They talked as they hadn't had the occasion to during their sessions at the massage class, and only peripherally at their date over dinner and the dance floor two weeks earlier. She asked about his two marriages, to whom, how long, how enduring, what continued between them, if anything, and how many other short- or long-term relationships had there been? He asked her about Oklahoma, her upbringing (she was a tomboy, she confided, and rode horses as a young girl, hoped eventually to settle somewhere she could own and stable a nice roan). He asked how she'd gotten into modern dance, and she told him she'd been forced into ballet lessons as a kid, but when she saw her first modern dance perfor-mance as a young teenager she was hooked. She told him about Jason, her blonde beau in Hawaii (they'd met when he'd sold her a surfboard), whom she'd been off-again, on-again with for years and with whom she was still planning to live when she went to Indiana two weeks from that evening (*"to see if it will work . . . or not"*). He told her about his teaching, how he'd loved his classes, how shocked he'd been when notified he was to be let go from the university, how much it had hurt and what a time he'd had, trying to find a serviceable job in the years since. She confessed she wanted eventually to settle somewhere in Oklahoma on a ranch and he admitted that despite his country upbringing he was determined to stay in New York, that here was where he felt writers needed to be, that he was no longer the country boy he'd recently written a series of poems about, already published as the centerfold of a magazine devoted exclusively to poetry.

"What do you like about me?" he asked at one point. "I mean, really?"

"I like that you're so smart," she said. "You've got all this learnin', and that impresses me, but at the same time, you're so down to earth. I feel almost out of my league, but I so admire that. Golly, a PhD! Wow! That took discipline!" She paused a moment. "The fact that you're big and good looking doesn't hurt, of course. No woman would object to that. But—you know what—what I like most is, you've just got . . . style!"

He laughed. "Style, eh? That's really interesting. You know, when I was a kid . . . eleven or twelve, maybe . . . an older cousin, from Oklahoma—Buford was his name— came to visit the family. He was about twenty, I believe.

Maybe older. I lived in a little place out back from the main house and so that's where they decided to stick him overnight. We talked quite a bit before we went to sleep that evening and he said to me—I'll always remember this—'Robert, makes no difference what you decide to do with your life, but whatever it is, do it with *style!*'" So, to hear you say that pleases me a great deal. Makes me think maybe I've succeeded, in that at least."

"In spades, buddy. Now, turnabout is fair play. What do you like about me?"

"Oh, my goodness! Well, start with the fact that you're pretty damned good-looking. You must know that. You're petite and I find petite women more attractive for some reason. Can't be my mother, she was five-seven, came from a tall family. Her father, the one we called 'Big Grandpa,' was a big old country boy who served as sheriff of that small town in Oklahoma for almost thirty years. Anyway, what else I like, I guess, is that you're a dancer. I admire that. I mean, talk about discipline! What you have to do to maintain that shape, that flexibility! And you're so focused, so lively. And straightforward. You say what you think. I like that, too. Also, I like that you obviously enjoy nature: stars, moon, all the rest of it."

So on they talked, alone on a roof in New York with the stars and the moon overhead creating light and beauty, at the same time that it encouraged a kind of dry ache in each of their hearts.

"I don't know, Dr. Fairweather," she said finally. "We like each other, I guess. Maybe a lot even, but I just don't know. About you and me, I mean. I mean, how? How, Robert? How on earth will those stars align for us, can you answer me that? Or should they? Should they at all?"

He was quiet a moment, then, after clearing his throat, said: "If nothing's really changed, which you told me earlier this evening, what led you to call and invite me over here?"

She looked at him almost in alarm, then looked away again.

"Because I missed you," she said finally. "Because I couldn't get you out of my mind."

He snorted. "I'm rather surprised. It's been two weeks since I last saw you or heard from you, so I'd assumed you'd forgotten me entirely. No longer in the picture. What changed your mind? Is this just a lark?"

"Shall I tell you?"

He looked at her inquiringly.

"It was when you kissed me at the bus stop. No, that's not it. It was when you put your tongue in my mouth."

He was shocked. "Really? I thought I'd blown it then. I thought, 'oh, shit, now I've gone and made a really stupid mistake.'"

"No, actually. It was unexpected, to be sure. But it was so . . . bold, so daring, so . . . masterful! I knew then that you wanted me. And like I said, I haven't been able to get that out of my mind."

He leaned toward her and kissed her then, pressed her head gently down to the pillow which lay behind her. Within minutes, on that star-sprinkled rooftop in Soho, they were making love.

"Oh, God!" she said, after it was all over, after their cries of passion had been shared with anyone in the neighborhood still awake and within hearing distance. "This is probably a big mistake, but I couldn't help myself. I needed you so much."

Robert stretched out beside her and smiled. "Don't fret it," he said. "You're not alone. As you've no doubt been able to tell, I needed it too."

"Hold me, Bobby."

A few minutes later, they made love again, more slowly this time, then fell asleep. When Robert awoke, as the silent day was just beginning to blossom, he gathered her into his arms and, carrying her down the stairs and into her apartment, tucked her into bed and stretched out alongside her, where once more he fell asleep.

When they awoke for good the next day around noon, they were timid around each other, uncertain. He didn't know whether to go or stay. Nor, it seemed, did she. But it was now Thursday and still no power, so they had time to spend together. As they were eating a bacon-and-eggs breakfast she'd cooked on her gas stove from stuff in her fridge, she finally said, "Shall we just enjoy the time we have left, then? Let's drive up to the Cape."

"The Cape?"

"The Cape. You wanna?"

He didn't know whether he wanted to or didn't. Everything seemed so up in the air. In the end, however, he agreed, reluctant to break it off.

It was a glorious summer day, not as hot as the day— or evening—before—the one in which a bolt of lightning in Westchester County had managed for an unknown number of hours to render dark the cultural capitol of the world, cast some of its population into an opportunistic mayhem from which it would likely take years to recover, and inexplicably create the opportunity for two solitary creatures' fraught but blissful moment. And because it was so beautiful, this brand new pair of wholly uncertain lovers managed to enjoy the drive: the breeze in the windows, the sunshine, the high, scudding clouds with no signs of rain. They decided, for reasons of cost, not to rent a cabin for their overnight stay, but to sleep in the car, thereby finally providing an answer to the age-old question: Can a six-foot, 190-pound man and a five-feet-two, 105-pound lady make love in the back seat of a Volkswagen beetle? Not altogether comfortably, it turns out but—whatthehell— orgasms are orgasms wherever they occur. And the two of them managed to laugh about it, as well.

On the trip home, however, they grew more silent.

Electrical power had returned in their absence; in that respect, the city had been restored. But little else was. When it came time for them to part, Robert smiled and held her tight, and she returned his embrace in spades. But it was over—they both knew it—so he said goodbye with a carefully marshaled nonchalance, knowing full well that his hijacked heart would take a long time to heal. Who knows? he thought as he exited her car in front of his building, perhaps it won't feel over until the next blackout rolls around.

Sixteen hundred stores looted. One thousand fires set. Thirty-seven thousand arrests made. All in one night. In the days and weeks that followed, Robert found little in the New York City newspapers—or for that matter, the national press—that could lift his dampened spirits. Things were far worse than what he'd witnessed along Myrtle Avenue. More looting and burning in Bedford-Stuyvesant and other parts of Brooklyn, at scattered locations in Harlem in Manhattan, and widely throughout the South Bronx. Clearly where the most disadvantaged people dwelled. Each time he read the results, he would wince and shake his head. Both the police and the fire department had been tasked with jobs far too vast to handle when they happened all at once, and in the dark. After each account he read, he would toss away the *New York Times* or *Time* or *Newsweek* and shake his head.

Which did nothing, of course, to relieve him of the need to earn a living. But whether it was his own attitude that was responsible (a significant want of hustle) or simply the fates conspiring against him, his career as a massage therapist proved to be short and insubstantial. He managed to service only three paying clients in the weeks that followed. Twice it was the same woman, and that proved to be Jackie's roommate, Stephanie, who'd heard lots about him and wanted to give it a try. (He would always wonder what parts she'd heard about but chose not to pry.) And the second time that he came to her place to perform the requested massage, a boyfriend (a man far older than Robert) was on hand to witness the event, carefully stroking his white handlebar moustaches as he looked on. Either because he didn't trust his almost naked cutie to be massaged while he wasn't around to watch or because he didn't trust his almost naked cutie to be massaged while he wasn't around to watch. (Robert had considered alternative explanations and just as quickly rejected them as so much hogwash.)

The third and last professional massage he gave was to the current girlfriend of his best friend, Mortimer. Samantha had requested this by proxy—Mortimer gave him the message—and he of course consented, avowing he would refuse to accept payment. But Samantha had insisted, and, in truth, he needed the money, so in the end he relented. The total earned from all three massages was $60. The price of the course he had taken to become a trained masseur was . . . $60. Well, he thought, at least he'd broken even.

And each evening thereafter, as he readied his chess pieces to be distributed to their assigned locations across the board in front of him, prepared for yet another lonely contest against himself, he would wonder aloud to his empty living room, "What in the fuck should I try next?"

EXTRA! EXTRA! READ ALL ABOUT IT!

ROBERT FAIRWEATHER BECAME eligible for six months unemployment compensation when he was axed by U. S. Customs & Marketing Federal Bank in mid-1978, having spent the better part of a year feverishly trying to learn the ropes in a position that—according to the CMFB's Personnel Department—had never actually existed in the first place. It had been, as one creepily confident Senior Vice President had put it to him one night when he was searching for a chair that had been stolen from his office, "a chimera." Thus cast adrift, he spent his waking hours veering between trying to write his first novel and studying books that followed the games of famous chess grandmasters, while once again becoming intimately familiar with the want-ad section of *The New York Times*.

Four months into this forced interregnum, his eyes alighted on an ad that seemed as if it might have been written with him in mind. The organization submitting the request wanted him (or at least the person they were trying to recruit) to start a newspaper. (Yes, a *newspaper*!) In a depressed New York City neighborhood. The contract was available for one year only, though it might be extended for a second. To Robert the project sounded both utterly intriguing and totally impossible. Its major drawback was that it paid only $10,000 for the entire year. Which was more than he was earning on unemployment (though not a lot) but substantially less than he'd been making at CMFB. (Which was, in turn, still less than he would have been making had he been paid for the job he was hired for—the one that, technically, did not exist.)

Whatever the case, the moment Robert first saw the ad he smiled and shook his head. "You've gotta be kidding," he muttered to himself. "It looks like they're asking for *me*. Who else would have an early journalism background like mine, however far back in the Dark Ages it might be? Who else would be crazy enough to aspire to something like this? And who else is dumb enough, or desperate enough, to try?"

He called immediately.

The source of the project's money turned out to be the federal government, through a program called CETA (Comprehensive Employment and Training Act) and the awardee of the contract was a non-profit community organization called PCH (Protection & Conservation of Housing). The neighborhood was Hell's Kitchen. Once home of the "Westies," one of New York's most notorious Irish gangs.

A week later, Robert crawled out of the nearest subway and walked west to 10ᵗʰ Avenue and 52ⁿᵈ Street. Pretty desolate. Nestled into a small, one-story building beside a corner filling station, a large hand-painted sign above its doorway, was PCH. He turned slowly, looking in each direction, before finally saying to himself, "Well, Fairweather. Welcome to the neighborhood. This is about as far away from U.S. Customs & Marketing Federal Bank as one can get."

Inside, he found a desk with a large, corpulent, jolly-looking Irish woman named Bridget, and to his right, in a corner office, already rising from her desk to greet him, a woman in her late forties who could have served as a stand-in for Margaret Thatcher. She shook his hand warmly but formally and invited him into her office. So far so good. As it turned out, she even spoke something like Ms. Thatcher, though he suspected it had more to do with private schools and Harvard than being brought up in Merry Old England. His instincts turned out to be correct. She lived on Fifth Avenue across from the Metropolitan Museum and her brother was an Executive Vice President of a major international bank. Fortunately, not CMFB.

"Welcome to PCH, Dr. Fairweather," she said. "I'm Millicent Millipede, and I'm Chairperson of the non-profit, Protection & Conservation of Housing. I found the resumé you sent me most fascinating and I'm eager to talk to you."

Before long they were conversing like buddies of long standing.

"So, let me get this straight," he said at last. "You're hoping to start a newspaper in a neighborhood where there's never been one? In Hell's Kitchen itself? Does that not strike you as rather ambitious?"

"Oh, without question!" she chirped in her deep and beautifully modulated voice. "We're a very ambitious organization. We've only been incorporated for two years but now we've been awarded this CETA grant, with its opportunity to hire several tenant organizers, a few community organizers and—the *pièce de resistance*—an editor for the newspaper we are planning to establish."

Robert nodded thoughtfully and looked away a moment. When his gaze returned to hers, he said, "And you expect to accomplish this while offering an editor only $10,000 a year?"

"Well, unfortunately, that salary is set by the federal government, which gave us the grant. It's a training program for community improvement, you see. There's no salary higher in this contract. Clearly, one has to do this job because one *wants to*, not because one hopes to become wealthy."

Or be utterly destitute, thought Robert. Like me.

"Clearly," he said. "Well, at least you've got a built-in advantage of some great name possibilities. *Hell's Kitchen Gazette. Hell's Kitchen Herald. Hell's Kitchen Mirror*! The choices are legion."

"Oh, dear no! The neighborhood has been re-christened "Clinton". The whole area—34th to 52nd streets, Eighth Avenue to the river—has been designated by the City as an 'improvement zone.' We're planning to call the newspaper—this was our secretary, Bridget's idea, she's a long-time neighborhood resident—*The Clinton Newspaper*."

Robert inwardly winced and thought, "Zounds! How utterly drab!" But he knew that wasn't a useful reaction, so he managed, "Ah! I see. Well, not too ear-catching, in my opinion. But not my decision to make, clearly. I certainly agree that it's an exciting idea, in any case."

Since in the past four months there hadn't been any job prospects he'd been remotely qualified for, he thought of all those empty pages in his bank book and declared himself interested. Which led to her assurance that, while she had one or two other candidates to interview, she was certain there was no one around who had half the qualifications that he did and if he wanted it, the job would be his. They shook hands and Robert left. Outside, he looked up and down the street and took a deep breath. "I don't know, Fairweather." he said aloud. "It may be chicken-feed, but at least it's a hedge against starvation."

He was barely though the screen door the first morning of his tenure at PCH when he was greeted by the secretary, Bridget, with the somewhat breathless news: "Did you see the piece in the *Daily News* today about evidence they found down along the railroad tracks that links a recent murder to one of the Westies? Our old neighborhood gang may still be around!"

Our gang? he thought. Neighborhood pride? "Uh, gosh, I somehow missed that! Don't often read the *Daily News*. Are you perhaps suggesting you think we should do a story on the Westies? In our first issue of *The Clinton Newspaper*?"

"Well, you're the editor of course, but I'm just saying . . . ."

"Why thank you, Bridget! Thanks very much. I'll look into it. But of course, our first issue is unlikely to be out before a month from now. Maybe longer. But that's certainly an exciting possibility. Thanks again!"

He did find the story—three inches on a back page— and it turned out to be a casual speculation by one detective about resemblance to a similar wipe-out several decades earlier. In Robert's reading, the detective's account made it appear a remote and tenuous possibility. He filed it in the back of his head as something to keep in mind, but wondered, "If she's so into that old Hell's Kitchen narrative, why would she name this venture something so sanitized as *The Clinton Newspaper*?

When summoned into Chairwoman Millipede's office later that day, he was told he'd been registered for a course in "community newsletters," a two-week half-day workshop beginning in a week's time. He murmured thanks and agreed, though it made him wonder whether her expectations for *The Clinton Newspaper* were lower than she'd let on?

Ray Dunlevy, the workshop's leader, turned out to be a tall, genial man with tufts of light brown hair circling his otherwise shiny pate and a rather extensive past in the newspaper game. Currently he edited the *Housing Authority Journal*, a full-size weekly newspaper with a circulation of 400,000 within New York's huge Housing Authority community. Earlier he'd done stints with both the Associated Press and *The Miami Herald*. Moreover, he'd gone to the Medill School of Journalism at Northwestern University, where Robert had been sent years earlier, for a five-week journalism workshop the summer between his junior and senior high school years.

They bonded immediately. And after the last session, Robert asked Ray if he might consent to serve on *The Clinton Newspaper*'s Board of Directors. Ray agreed, and when Robert reported this to Millicent, so did she.

Four weeks into Robert's new editorial job, little else had taken place to make the newspaper a reality. But finally, the other positions had been filled. There was Luke Esterhazy, a six-foot-three, skinny, twenty-something tenant organizer, with floppy brown hair he was forever brushing out of his face. Fresh out of college, and bursting with enthusiasm, Luke came at everything with a decidedly radical point of view. Also hired was Angie Papadopoulos, she of the frizzy, dishwater-blonde hair, an experienced tenant organizer and closer to thirty than the rest. There was Serena Lopez, a very pretty graduate student with dark, Colombian eyes that matched her ebony, shoulder-length tresses, starting her first job as community organizer—sweet, pleasant and always ready to help. And a few more tenant organizers, all under thirty. Robert, at forty-three, had already begun to feel old.

Once the hiring was accomplished, Chairwoman Millipede called the first staff meeting. Then, having greeted and introduced the staff members, she surprised Robert by asking him to "lay out his plans" for the newspaper.

Plans? he thought. I should have plans already? Oh, dear God. How could I make plans when I don't have any staff? He cleared his throat and tried to imagine himself in front of a more familiar audience, say an incoming class of freshmen. Which inadvertently recalled to him his very first day teaching. It was a Western Civilization course at Brooklyn Quintessential University. His briefcase packed with the required texts and syllabi, he'd strode confidently through the building's hallways, found the classroom, swung wide the door and, with a dramatic flourish, flipped on the overheads to proclaim, "Let there be *light*!" Next, he began to unpack all the texts he'd stuffed into his bag. Whereupon a student in the front row—a puzzled look on his face—interrupted him. "Professor?" he said. "Those all seem to be *history* books, and this is a class in *biology*. Are you sure you have the right room?"

He coaxed his mind back to the present moment.

"Well, this is a brand-new gig for me, as it likely is for all of us. From my perspective, I'd like to say, one of the first things we need to decide on is content. What's our *Clinton Newspaper* going to say? What stories do we cover? Let me tell you where I'm coming from at this moment; then I'd like to hear your suggestions.

"The way I see it, PCH is a housing organization and so the focus, in the early days, should be about landlord-tenant relations, identifying problem buildings and so on. Which means it's up to you guys to come up with the goods. The info. You'll be the first to identify these problems and so I'll count on you to give me a heads-up on what you think would make a good story. And I think it's important as well to remember that this is a *neighborhood* newspaper—or that's what we hope it will become—and so those of you who live here and know a lot about the neighborhood—not me, I live in Brooklyn, for God's sake—I'm depending on you to suggest events of interest as you learn about them. Whenever you hear, alert me, so we can be prepared. Can plan."

He looked quickly around the table. "I encourage all of you to come up with ideas for stories. And features. Subjects of interest that may change from month to month or week to week. I've recently become aware, for example, that there's the Ninth Avenue Festival. A really big deal from what I understand. And it happens in May. But there must be others. Hey! We could include a calendar! A list of local places of interest. Places to eat, places to go to the movies or to 'recreate' in whatever ways the neighborhood offers. Parks, maybe? And if we don't have enough parks, maybe that's something we should advocate for. You'll know that better than I."

He cast his eyes around the table.

"So, you should be prepared that I'm likely to ask you to write some of these stories. Somebody has to! If—or when—I do, don't be afraid, even if you don't think writing is your strong suit. I'm the editor and I'm here to help. So, those of you who know the neighborhood best, I'm counting on you. This is not a one-man band. It can't be. I'll need all the help I can get. It won't work unless everybody pitches in."

He stopped, looked around, waited. The phrase, *the silence was deafening*, tiptoed through his mind.

Just then Serena chimed in. "I may be able to do some translating into Spanish. If that's needed."

"Great!" Robert responded. "Thank you for your offer, Serena! We'll no doubt be calling on you."

And the meeting moved on, Millicent encouraging each to give some sense of what they thought was expected of them. Their responses made Robert think of pulling teeth.

In the following days, things still seemed to crawl. Robert felt like he was being asked to assemble a jigsaw puzzle when the major pieces were still missing. He finally concluded that, if stories were written, he'd have to write them. If ads were sold, in an effort to eventually become self-sustaining, he'd need to sell them. If photos were to accompany the stories—essential for a newspaper—someone would have to take them. Where would he find these people? And how could he shake off the loner he'd been most of his life?

Fortunately for his project there was also Brother Lochinvar, not a PCH hire but a roaming Jesuit priest with an open, friendly disposition. Brother L lived locally and was one of the kindest, most selfless persons Robert had ever been around. Almost spookily so. He seemed to know everyone in the neighborhood and was always ready to lend a hand. He had somehow developed a relationship with PCH and Millicent, and volunteered to be of help however he could.

Knowing the neighborhood now seemed a priority. Millicent had included money in the budget for tree-planting to beautify Tenth Avenue. In cooperation with the City, PCH was to choose the locations; so Millicent suggested Robert team up with Serena to accomplish this. Thus, Serena became his early guide. They meandered the length of the avenue choosing locations. Chatting and kibitzing with this attractive Colombian along the journey, Robert developed what he hoped might be an enduring friendship. And later she turned out to be an adept translator of selected stories into Spanish.

He learned even more about the neighborhood, however, from Brother L, who knew the environs (and its denizens) as no one else did.

"I want to introduce you to someone," he said on their first walk. "A woman who's always in her front window, looking out on her neighbors, who daily stop by to chat. Her name's Mae Moriarty. Some people think she's a saint."

(*A saint?* Robert wondered. Careful. At first blush, a few had thought the same about Rasputin.)

They found Mae—just as Brother L had said—perched at a front window of her apartment. She had a full, round face, large shoulders, a kind of doughy body, a high forehead, and short but abundant grey hair parted on the left and falling gracefully along the right. A glass of orange juice sat in front of her. She smiled at him.

Robert had once had a Jewish girlfriend whom he sometimes helped light candles on a Friday evening. He was instantly convinced that this woman could light candles with only her smile.

"This is a really nice area," she said following introductions. "I've been here oh so many years and know almost everyone in the neighborhood."

"Nice to make your acquaintance as well," said Robert. "Brother L tells me you occupy a very special place in these surroundings."

"Oh, you'd be surprised how nice the people are in this vicinity," she said. "I've never met anyone here I didn't like."

"And how did you come to occupy this particular perch?" he pressed. "You just like people? And fresh air?"

"Oh, I *do*!" she said. "I like everyone I meet around here. I've been sitting in this window for the last twenty years. I was paralyzed when I was just a young girl, and this is a way I can still interact with my friends and neighbors. I have a cousin and a niece who come over to help me out." She sipped her orange juice. "I'm never lonely. I feel lucky. I wouldn't live anywhere else if you paid me a million dollars."

As they walked on, Robert confided to Brother L, "Well, she's something all right. I don't know much about sainthood, but I'd certainly agree she's special."

Further afield, he found there was a lot more to discover about the Hell's Kitchen neighborhood. Many old and well-known churches—Sacred Heart, Holy Cross, St. Clément's, and the Russian Orthodox Church of St. Cyril & Methodius. Hell's Kitchen also hosted most of the theatre district: theatres large and small, plus the famous East-West Restaurant Row, which fed all those playgoers both before and after the shows. And locations where movies had once been made as well as others where TV shows were currently produced and aired.

But mostly, on the walks he would take during his noon hours, as he became more familiar with the neighborhood, he observed the housing, dominated row after row by Old Law Tenements. Built during the nineteenth century, most had never been revised from their original floor plans, with their tiny windows, narrow spaces and original claw-footed bathtubs still resting in the middle of their kitchens.

So, as weeks passed, some moments were fun; others continued to be like trying to tie a knot in a rope that kept fraying in your hands. Early on, while struggling to get a good quote for an article about housing and tenants, having asked tenant organizer Luke Esterhazy could he please give him a quote about a particular part of a housing effort Luke had been deeply involved in, he received only the reply, "Shucks, I wouldn't know what to say."

After a moment, contemplating defeat or, at best, a flavorless article, Robert had scrawled a sentence on his yellow pad and called out across the room, "Say, Luke, can you come here a moment?"

When Luke appeared at his desk a minute or two later, he handed him his pad.

"Luke, do me a favor. Would you read what's written there?"

Luke furrowed his brow, mumbled "sure," and began to read. Silently.

"Uh, no, Luke," Robert interrupted. "I mean, read it aloud."

"Oh, okay," said Luke. He did so.

"Now," said Robert. "Do you agree with that? Is that something that *you* might say about the situation in that apartment building? Where tenants are struggling with their landlord to escape eviction? Would you endorse that statement? That idea?"

Luke furrowed his brow and thought. "Well, yeah," he said finally. "Sure. I agree with it."

"And you have just read it out loud, so I can accurately say, 'you said it'. Correct?"

"I suppose so. What's the point?"

"Well, Luke, I told you I needed a quote about that dispute, and you've just provided it. So, let me ask you officially, 'May I quote you? In this article? May I write in this story that will soon appear in the newspaper that 'Luke Esterhazy said this'?"

Luke smiled. "Oh, I get it. Sure. You can quote me."

"Great! Thanks, Luke!"

In December of that year, dressed as smartly as he and his bank account were capable of, Robert stood on the sidewalk in front of the broad steps of the Metropolitan Museum of Art, gazing across the street. He'd been a visitor at the Met many times, but never inside an apartment in that prized and expensive real estate across Fifth Avenue. Yet that was where Millicent Millipede lived, on the fourteenth floor. *No! Correction!* The fourteenth and fifteenth floors! His employer was having a Christmas party. Chairwoman Millipede was the hostess, and it should just be getting underway in *her digs.*

Gauging the traffic carefully, he trotted across the street, dodging and feinting to avoid becoming a statistic.

It was not Millicent but a butler—sparse-haired, tall, and with what seemed like an almost military posture—who opened the door, bowing slightly, gesturing Robert in with a broad sweep of his arm.

Robert introduced himself.

"Of course! Please come in, Mr. Fairweather. Merry Christmas! May I take your wrap? Guests and the refreshments are to my right, if you would please. Later on, when you're ready to leave, just ask for Horace, and I'll fetch your outer garments for you."

Christmas music by talented choristers came from somewhere.

"Thank you, Horace," he said. "And Merry Christmas to you!"

Horace smiled and gestured once more toward the next room. "Many guests have already arrived."

Robert spun round to face the indicated room but drew up short. On the wall dead ahead was a painting which he recognized as an Edward Hopper. And on an adjacent wall . . . a Vermeer! Was that even possible? Damn! How rich was this lady? Or did she just walk across the street to the Met and borrow a few canvases each time she had a party?

His hostess, stylishly arrayed in a floor-length black gown, a silver tiara in her hair, stood near a table laden with a huge cut-glass punch bowl; behind her a dramatically copious selection of liquors and cordials arrayed like Christmas candy along a separate table. While talking to a man Robert didn't recognize, she caught his eye and beckoned him over. He spotted Luke Esterhazy a few paces away, chatting with a very elegant Serena.

"Merry Christmas, Millicent," he said as he drew near.

"To you as well, dear heart. Robert, this is my brother, Kenneth. Ken's an EVP at Dow Jones Rolling Stock Bank. Bro, this is Robert Fairweather, the editor of the brand-new newspaper my non-profit is creating." They exchanged greetings and smiles. A younger brother, he guessed. Late forties, perhaps? If Millicent was a Margaret Thatcher lookalike, this guy was a grown-up Lord Fauntleroy.

"What a splendid apartment you have here, Millicent," Robert said. "Did I just spot a Hopper and a Vermeer in the next room? Do you just borrow them from that place across the street whenever you want?" (Then he winced at his own cheeky attempt at humor.)

"Yes, you did, and no I don't," she said coquettishly. "They're like dear friends to me now; I've had them so many years. Listen, Robert, if you're an art lover, there are more paintings, and you're quite welcome to give yourself a complete tour. Including upstairs. The stairwell is just through that door and to your right. But now, please, dear heart, get yourself a drink and enjoy the party! It's Christmastime!"

After treating himself to a double Glen Livet single malt

over ice, he joined Luke and Serena, while waving hello to Angie and—was that her husband?—a few paces further along. A moment later, after Luke departed to join another group, Robert flashed a very appraising smile at Serena.

"Wow, Serena, you look terrific!" he said. "Stunning, in fact!"

Her silk dress was of a gentian blue with doohickeys strewn over it that made it sparkle in the lights. (Sequins, were they?) The bodice was cut so that the upper half of her breasts were charmingly visible, while her raven tresses were swept up into a do he'd never seen before. Half her hair was gathered loosely into a swirling bun, with long strands snaking dramatically down to frame her face before drifting even lower, coming at last to rest against her bosom. Her eyes danced merrily. "Why, thank you, Robert," she said, with a little curtsy. "You look rather nice yourself."

"Sweet of you to say, oh, elegant one. But I'm afraid it's the difference between 'presentable' and 'Holy Shit! Looka that!' You belong on the red carpet at Oscar time."

She giggled.

They talked a few minutes longer and then drifted apart, into other groupings. Half an hour later, however, they wound up together again in a corner.

"Listen," he said. "I don't know if you noticed those paintings in the front hall, but Millicent tells me there's more art in other rooms. Upstairs, particularly. I'd love to see them. Would you like to accompany me? That stairway takes us to the next level. Or would you rather just find some Mistletoe and make out?"

She laughed and slapped his arm playfully. "The paintings sound like fun! I love art. My family in Colombia owns some nice pieces too."

That was a surprise.

They refreshed their drinks (another double for Robert) and gaily swept up the heavily carpeted staircase.

What they encountered was, they both agreed, rather breathtaking. Starting with the spiral staircase and the tasteful, deep-pile carpets everywhere. But the paintings! The engravings! The etchings! All handsomely done, in different styles and from different periods. Nothing more from the Northern Renaissance, but there were Van Goghs, Cézannes, Picassos (sketches only), several Dufys, and others that neither of them had ever heard of. Robert found himself impressed with the depth of Serena's appreciation.

"My family doesn't have a collection as memorable as this, of course," she said, after the fourth room they'd entered, "and certainly not as valuable. But both my mother and my father love art. He even painted a bit himself. He is much too busy, of course, to devote a lot of time to it."

"What does your father do?"

"A physician. In Bogotá. A psychiatrist, in fact. And my mother is involved in a lot of charities. They're both wonderful people."

"Sounds like."

After a moment, she said, "Robert, no more for me, I think. I should go. I need to get some rest."

"And me as well," he said.

He looked into her eyes, felt himself momentarily lost. He set his glass down on a nearby small table, took her hands in his. "I'd be happy to see you back to your apartment," he said.

She smiled and looked away.

"Robert, no. I really like you. And admire you so much. What you've done, what you're doing now, with the newspaper. You are a very interesting man. But I am engaged. My fiancé is still in Bogotá, finishing his last courses in architecture. When that's done, next year he will join me here and we will be married."

He nodded. "Of course," he said. "How could it be otherwise? Besides, you're 24 and I'm . . . well, past 40. Still, I can't help being attracted to you. You're a lovely woman, in more ways than one. Your fiancé is a very lucky man."

"Will you walk me out now? Put me in a cab? And I will see you Monday?"

"Sounds like a plan," he said. "Time to call Horace."

No follow-up, Robert kept telling himself, over and over on the train home, after he'd found a cab for Serena. None. *Nada. Don't dwell on a hopeless affair of the heart!* he commanded himself. He'd had them before, hadn't he? Wasn't that an advantage of his age? And at PCH headquarters the following Monday, as well as the next day and the next and the next, the two of them might smile at each other as if sharing some private joke, but that was it.

And as work on the paper continued, on into January, February and beyond, he managed to bring out several issues, even pushed a few others to try their hand at writing stories. But selling ads remained his principal dilemma. No one seemed interested; each seemed to think it was none of their affair. Which left it to Robert and, each time he journeyed out to solicit them, he'd find himself quickly growing testy and hard on himself. "Jesus!" he would think as he trudged along the streets, poking his nose into this pub or that cleaners, "I've already proved to myself that I couldn't sell shoes worth a damn—quite beautiful ladies' shoes that customers can hold in their hands and examine!—and now I'm expected to peddle something as abstract as advertising? In a newspaper that barely exists?"

His only success on that score—and this was later in the year—was landing a half-page ad from a huge real-estate developer, Simon Dunst, who had substantial holdings in Clinton. And way before the issue in which that was to appear, news of that sale brought forth an argument from his fellow PCH-ers. In a Board meeting both Luke and Angie were ready to tar and feather him for "selling out" to a developer. "We're on the side of housing and tenants!"

they clamored at him during a board meeting, "not land-lords and developers! For shame!"

Troubled though he was by the ferocity of their objections, Robert held firm. "I promise you," he said. "I have accepted money for this newspaper-to-be, to help finance its creation and continuity. But I will never be guided by anything he or another advertiser has to say about what I do or do not print. That's a promise."

All the way home on the subway that evening, he mulled over the argument he'd had with his fellow employees, wondering whether editors of current metropolitan newspapers still adhered to standards that had been drilled into him so long ago. How successful were they, if so? How firm, how principled? He would scarcely have thought about these things, he decided, were it not for having, rather accidentally, been re-injected into journalism through this fledgling attempt to start a newspaper from scratch, which, if he were to seriously speculate about its long-run success, was probably doomed. But he remained, he realized, committed to the principles that had been established as long ago as John Peter Zenger's 1735 trial, wherein he was successfully defended by Alexander Hamilton after being accused of libel, the earliest example of the principle that "if it's the truth, it can't be libel."

And after dinner, as he was laying out his chess pieces to resume his nightly games against himself, just before placing his king's rook in its accustomed starting place, he paused and chuckled. He'd just remembered a clarion call he'd heard uttered over the radio as a teenager, one that still moved him: "The power and the freedom of the press is a flaming sword. Use it justly, hold it high, guard it well."

A NEW BEGINNING

"TODAY IS SO great!" said Serena, smiling. "I'm really enjoying this."

"Very satisfying," said Robert. "I'm glad we were able to bring it out on time. And it's a good issue, I think."

On a warm Saturday in May in the late nineteen-seventies Robert Fairweather, a 44-year-old ex-academic, sat in an open booth at Manhattan's Ninth Avenue Festival, surrounded by copies of *The Clinton Newspaper*. Beside him was Serena Lopez, a stunning, black-tressed young Colombian. Both were dressed in shorts and tee shirts. Robert was the newspaper's editor and Serena, a 24-year-old graduate student, had translated several of the included stories into Spanish. The newspaper was an experiment, part of the effort by a non-profit organization called Protection and Conservation of Housing. Each had been hired in the fall of the previous year through a federal grant seeking to improve the quality of life in the neighborhood commonly known as Hell's Kitchen, which New York City had rechristened Clinton. The federal program was known as CETA (Comprehensive Employment and Training Act). The goal of both the City and of PCH was to rejuvenate a neglected neighborhood.

The issue Robert and Serena were distributing had been printed two days earlier; its lead story was about the festival itself. The bottom of the front page featured an artist's conception of a stretch of Ninth Avenue. It showed outdoor tables featuring Chinese music, curried rice, Thai food, children's games, souvlaki, jugglers, clams & beer, jewelry, watermelon, and hand-woven scarves among many other goodies, along with footprints leading potential visitors from one table to another. It was accurate enough; almost all the dozens of restaurants along this wide boulevard, each with its own ethnic flavor—Irish, French, Italian, Mexican, Indian—packed cheek by jowl for over a mile, had transferred their wares this day to booths along the street, in the midst of games and bands and step-dancing and hawkers of tee shirts and tube socks and wood-and-shell necklaces and more.

Robert and Serena had eagerly volunteered to tend the booth at the launch of the two-day festival. Aside from displaying this issue of the newspaper on the table, they had each spent enjoyable moments strolling up and down the bustling boulevard, hawking their wares: free newspapers for the throngs of smiling passersby who'd come to Manhattan's most famous street fair.

But there was another aspect to Robert's enjoyment of the day. He had a not-so-secret crush on Serena, which had been both acknowledged and declared inoperable back at the PCH Christmas party the previous December.

"I'm loving your stories on the history of the neighborhood," said Serena. What Clinton was like through the ages."

"Thanks. Fun to write. Fun to research."

He smiled, as a young man dressed in a hobo outfit and wearing clown makeup came staggering by on a pair of stilts.

"You'd never catch me on top of those," said Serena.

"Me neither. Not now, anyway. But back in the day . . . . Say, pretty lady, did I ever tell you about the time I was a clown for the Ringling Brothers Barnum & Bailey circus?"

She turned to look at him with a frown of infinite doubt on her face. "Oh, sure, *Doctor* Fairweather," she said.

"I did! I did!" he said. "Scout's honor!" He raised his right hand as if in testimony.

"You were a Boy Scout?"

His shoulders slumped. "Not really. That's just an expression. Though I was a Cub Scout for a while . . . but *hey*, that's not the point. I really, actually, absolutely performed as a clown. Briefly."

"I can't believe it," she said. "Is there anything you haven't done? Or tried? So tell me."

He scratched his small blonde beard, remembering.

"Well, it was many years ago when I was still a very broke graduate student." He snickered, shook his head as if to clear it.. "As opposed to a very broke ex-history professor. Oh, well.

"Anyway, I noticed in the *Times* that the circus was holding a contest, with a fifty-dollar prize—that's what I was after, of course—and so I applied. I didn't have any clown costume and no fake nose or fake hair, or anything like that. So I figured I'd have to improvise. I found among my few possessions some red tape with which I fashioned some eyebrows and used white shoe polish on my hair and beard, painted myself a big red mouth with lipstick an ex-girlfriend had left behind, and showed up at the audition having designed a little improvised routine involving a skillet—that's an item I brought from home—and some imaginary pancakes. There were only three contestants, and one was terrible, but the other, unfortunately, had managed to procure a clown costume from somewhere. Along with clown white, fake orange hair, the whole bit. I thought his routine was unimpressive, and mine was much cleverer. I basically mimed cooking pancakes and tossing them up in the air where the last one completely disappears and I'm wandering all over, eyes cast to the skies, when the lost pancake—plop!—hits me in the face. They later said mine was 'awfully creative' and the decision might have been different if I'd been able to do it in a more traditional clown costume. So, no good. I'd spent my last five dollars on a jar of cold cream, so I was broker than before."

Serena looked at him, her beautiful face contorted with skepticism.

"Believe it or not, they later got in touch to ask if I'd represent Ringling Brothers in the Labor Day Parade in New York. I guess the other guy was performing with the circus somewhere. Or he could have died already. I don't know. Probably died from an overdose of pancake makeup."

She shook her head. "Robert, you are just too much."

"How true, how true," he said. "And you can have me for free, so what are you waiting for?"

Serena laughed and slapped him gently on the shoulder. "I think you're remarkable," she said. "But you know I mustn't go there." She leaned over and gave him a buss on the cheek.

He looked at her. A beauty. *My Colombian beauty! No, no*, he chided himself. *That other dude's Colombian beauty. Her Colombian fiancée, the architect, in his last year of study back in Bogotá. So, hands off! But it would be fine. So, so fine.*

"I know, I know," he said. "That one kiss will have to do. But do you mind if I don't wash my face for a week?"

From a rocky start, little by little, The *Clinton Newspaper* had grown. The first two issues had been in newsletter format; later issues were all tabloids. When Robert had been hired as editor, no other staff had yet been hired. He was expected to start the enterprise from scratch and—so it appeared— all by himself, since the nine other employees covered by the CETA grant were community organizers and tenant organizers. No writers, no journalist wannabes. Nothing. Robert had finally managed to find and cajole photographers to take pictures to accompany some stories, which at first were all written by him. Gradually, by hook or by crook, he'd recruited others among the PCH staff to pitch in. And a few to use their community contacts to sell ads, which Robert hated and was terrible at doing.

And eventually, the paper had grown. He now featured a box on the front page, listing "ON THE INSIDE . . . ." There were notices of workshops and courses, tips for seniors, a community calendar, articles about neighborhood improvements and activities, about clamorous City Council meetings that affected the housing in the neighborhood, about the role of private developers in Clinton. There were editorials (which he enjoyed writing). And each issue would add to a series of articles on the history of the neighborhood—it had become his favorite piece to write—which took him deep into the archives of the New York Historical Society. (This was the one aspect in which he felt that the old Robert Fairweather—the history scholar—and the new Fairweather—the editor—had joined together.)

And so it continued. He assigned the stories; he designed the pages, sometimes with the input of others; he blocked it out; he decided on size and placement of the photographs; he proofread; it was his baby. Each issue was more attractive, he felt, than the last. Slowly, over many months, he began to feel a bit of pride in his stewardship. It was the first time since his forced departure from Brooklyn Quintessential University in 1971 that he could remember feeling that.

Still. Living on $10,000 a year was a strain. A strain, he kept asking himself, or an impossibility? It might have been doable, he thought, if he still resided in Oklahoma, his childhood home, or some backwoods holler in the Ozarks. But this was New York! All those years since he'd lost his position teaching Russian History just as the bottom had fallen out of the academic market had been a financial strain and he could feel himself slipping ever deeper into a hole. He'd tried bartending, driving a taxi, typing, selling shoes, banking, tried halving his rent by taking in a room-mate; nothing had worked. And approaching soon was the date when his beloved Columbia University's graduate student loans would come due and would need to be repaid. Six thousand bucks. *On top of what I already owe on my credit cards?* Sitting at home of an evening with a lone beer and his chess pieces, he would grow morose and wonder: What's next for me, hey? Debtor's prison? The PCH contract, he'd recently learned, would likely be extended for a second year, but was that even remotely acceptable? Another $10,000 for the year? More like another $10,000 in the hole.

Sitting at his desk at PCH while doodling on a yellow pad, Robert thought: perhaps it was a mistake to have given up on having roommates to share the rent burden? But his final experience with a roommate had impressed upon him how problematic that situation could become. His decision to quash that stream of money came about this way: he'd accepted as a tenant a young woman who seemed nice enough at first—to be honest, she was never *not* nice—but being thrown together in such intimate circumstances had revealed unforeseen difficulties. Namely, she had quite early on (in fact, their first night together) given him to understand that she would be more than willing to make him the source of her sexual satisfaction if he would be so kind as to grant her the same favor. And Robert, who had felt starved for sex for the better part of a year, allowed himself to acquiesce to her overture. In fact—it must be said—with some enthusiasm. Very soon, he could not deny, it was no longer clear who was the acquies*cer* and who was the acquies*cee*. Yet he and his new roommate (her name was Phoebe) soon discovered they had nothing in common beyond their voracious appetites and thus each found themselves complaining bitterly that the situation was flawed at its root. For a brief period, however, each decision to cease and desist from their mutual pleasuring, no matter how sincere, would lead only to an equally mutual honing of their respective appetites, the end result being they would succumb with an even greater intensity and more tumultuous activity than before. It proved the better part of two months before they could wean themselves away from addiction to each other's yearnings sufficiently to end their arrangement for good, and part company. So with two furrowed brows and much gnashing of teeth, they finally managed to cut the cord. Which meant, in its turn, that following Phoebe's departure, Robert had been left with the same money problems as before.

In the middle of a second heat wave, as the summer drew to a close, Robert spotted a story in *The Chief*, the New York City civil service newspaper, that tests were soon forthcoming for a position called *Staff Analyst* in any number of City departments. He'd never considered working for the City before, but he now began to ask himself, why not? The position paid $16,000/yr. if you (a) passed the test and (b) having been interviewed, were hired. And once you were a civil servant, he'd heard, it was difficult to be cut loose. Comparative security. So, he considered it. The test was on a Saturday in September. As an ex-academic with rather broad knowledge, Robert had always had an edge with tests.

On the Friday before Saturday's exam, he knocked on the PCH Chairperson's door and she waved him in.

"Millicent"— Millicent Millipede, the very nice and staggeringly rich woman who'd grown a conscience and founded PCH—"I think it's important for you to know that this Saturday I'm planning to take a civil service exam for a possible position with the City. It might not even work out, you know. I could flunk the test and not be called. It's exploratory. But I thought I owed it to myself . . .."

"Robert, dear heart, of course! You must do what you think is best for you! I never expected our association to last forever, and I'm terribly grateful for all you've already done. I know the salary here is a huge financial strain on everybody and I thank you for finding the time to share your skills with us. Just keep me informed, if you will, as much in advance as you can, whenever you do decide."

"I certainly will, Millicent. But I think it would be best if no one else knows at this point? Until something definite comes about? If it does."

"Quite so. Quite so." She made a motion as if zipping her mouth. "Mum's the word. And again, whatever your decision, thank you awfully for your service up to now."

Three weeks after he'd taken the test—busy weeks dominated by work on the next issue of the paper—he was informed he'd passed; in fact, he'd been among the top finishers. No information was immediately available as to when the "shape-up," as it was referred to—the gathering where all these individual departments of City government conducted interviews for the available jobs—was to take place. So he held his peace. And waited.

In early October, when Issue No. 6 of the newspaper was ready to be put to bed, he scheduled time with the printers to bring the copy down to their offices in Soho and finalize the product. On the Friday before the Saturday he would travel to the printers—a press in Soho—he was told by Millicent that Sheila Shelailey, the neighborhood resident who'd been recently chosen by her to be Chair of *The Clinton Newspaper's* Board, had asked could she come along to help?

Robert had misgivings. Mainly because he doubted Sheila's ability to help much. However deeply she yearned for the position as Chair, she lacked any kind of relevant experience. True, she'd written the lead story about the Street Fair back in May's issue of the paper (she'd volunteered), but her skills were so rudimentary that she'd needed a lot of editing. She claimed she was looking forward to a career as a journalist, but this had been her only exposure to the craft. And this was the woman who'd been chosen as the Chairperson?

But with the certain knowledge that his boss approved, Robert did the mental equivalent of shrugging his shoulders. After all, Millicent had argued (and she wasn't wrong), that the whole point of the contract was to create a *neighborhood* newspaper, so finding a board chairman who was both from the neighborhood and "interested in journalism" was an important step.

So, the next morning he and Sheila traveled to the printers together and were ushered into the small workroom where last-minute decisions about putting the paper to bed were made.

"So, this is where it all gets done," she said.

Robert nodded. "This is where the rubber meets the road. It's where what up to now is just individual stories and pictures and columns and editorials and such—all of which we call *copy*—gets set in appropriate typefaces, fitted into the predetermined number of pages, and becomes a newspaper."

At first the work went well enough. He gave Sheila a few column inches to proofread as each came back from the printer, even though he was pretty sure he'd need to proof them again.

Then a problem arose over a question of the lengthy housing story in Spanish. Serena had translated the story and Robert had every confidence in her, but still, every story needed to be proofread. He'd taken high school Spanish and had some experience in both reading and speaking it then and later, but, although he was confident he could do a satisfactory job, he certainly couldn't do it at warp speed.

Then a second problem emerged from that: the article's length. Written Spanish occupies more space than English. He explained this to the printing company's vice president when he came in to ask what was taking so much time and the man nodded, shrugged his shoulders and left. But how to fix this? Should something—say a paragraph—be cut? Could it be cut without damaging the story or short-sighting the article and its author? Would Spanish readers object, and with cause? He sought in vain for a solution.

Could the same paragraphs be ripped from each? It would mean more work for him, and then more for the printers.

"Why don't you reduce the half-page ad the Spanish story is above?" asked Sheila.

Robert looked. It was Solomon Dunst's ad, the one he himself had procured. The only half-page ad that anyone had ever sold. He'd been dogged by others at PCH about it, in fact, because theirs was an organization sympathetic to tenants while Dunst was a developer. Robert had needed to persuade them that he would never allow Dunst to influence what he brought into print. He heaved a sigh.

"Can't really do that," he said. "He paid for a half-page; he should get a half-page. Our problem shouldn't be his problem. He should get what he paid for."

"He's a *developer*!" she said huffily. "A real-estate mogul! We're not in favor of his policies. Hell, we're not even in favor of his *species*! We're a protector of housing!"

Robert laughed at her species reference but held firm. "Doesn't matter," he said. "My word is my word."

Then he frowned and, after a couple of seconds, said, "Listen, you want to do me a favor? Call Millicent and see if she can scare up Dunst's phone number."

Fifteen minutes later, while Robert continued to work, she managed to get the number and, at his behest, she called him. Then she handed the phone to Robert, and he briefed Dunst on the problem. "It will mean about a quarter-inch loss over each of four columns," he said. "It's still a big ad and extremely noticeable. But it is a smidgen less than a full half-page."

"No worries," said Dunst. "We'll be fine."

Robert heaved a sigh of relief and put down the phone. "Okay, it's a go," he said.

Just then one of the printers returned to their little workroom and raised his eyebrows in silent interrogation. Robert smiled and handed him the copy, explaining what he'd need to do with the ad. "You can now go ahead with it," he said. "We're done."

The minute the door closed, however, Sheila said, "Hold on a minute. I think there's something else we need to discuss. Remember we noticed that huge water-main break just as we arrived today?"

"Yeah, a real bummer. It'll be somebody's big story, for sure. Too bad we're not able to respond quickly enough to cover it."

"I think it's too big a story to ignore. We should rip out some of our stories and cover this instead."

"Sheila! Are you nuts! We're not a *daily* newspaper. Right now, we're more akin to a monthly than the weekly we aspire to become. We can't even predictably publish every *month* yet."

"I say we go there now. Rip out our headlines and write up the story of the water-main break. This is our community and our community newspaper."

"What about resources, Sheila? We have no staff! Who's

gonna write the story? Who's gonna make all those calls to the City Planning department and Transportation and the Mayor's office and Con Ed and the private contractors and any other city agency that has some piece of this? Who's gonna interview those working stiffs out there trying to get it under control? There's a lot of information to be ferreted out. You'd need three or four reporters working simultaneously on different parts of the story to make it feasible. And you'd need your own printing press. Because we've kept these guys working overtime already. They've been very nice about our slowness but . . . no, we just can't do it, Sheila. Like it or don't, this is our only shot at getting this issue of *The Clinton Newspaper* out at all."

She pouted, then shot back, "Well, I'm the Chair of the Board! I'm the publisher. You're just the editor. So, I'm going to overrule you."

Robert looked at her in astonishment. After a moment, he said quietly, "Let's just think this through a moment, Sheila. With all due respect, you still have a lot to learn about journalism and about newspapers. Now I don't know how much you know about me. I was not hired because I was a former Russian history professor. I was hired because a long, long time ago I was planning a career in journalism. I'd had lots of experience in high school and had studied journalism at Northwestern University during the summer between my junior and senior years. I went to college on a journalism scholarship, something you might think about for yourself one day.

"So please, listen to me. True, you're the Chairperson and Publisher. But when the paper is being put to bed, I'm in control. The time for arguing about what goes in and what stays out is past. Tomorrow, Monday, or whenever we have our next board meeting, you can ask the board to fire me if you like. But when the paper is being put to bed, the editor is in charge. That's just the way it is. Sorry."

He looked at his watch. "It's now 9:30. We've been here all day. We were only expected to be here until 4:00 pm. Let's go home and get some sleep, okay?" He nodded his head toward the print shop. "We've distressed these guys long enough."

It looked like a wide sea churning with fish. So many tables with so many white tablecloths and, surrounding each, this school of sockeyes, leaping over each other hoping to be noticed. Hard to believe these were actually people! But they were, and each one searching for a job.

Two minutes after entering the door, Robert ambled through the confusion, wondering where he should go first. How many city departments were there? Plenty, obviously. He looked around for a table where candidates were fewest and discovered one where there was no one at all, except for the interviewer. He approached cautiously. Was he headed for the Department of Funerals, perhaps? The Department of Molecular Disintegration?

The sign above the table said Department of Housing: Past, Present, Future, and under that, the letters BPMA. The man behind the table, a fellow in his late fifties, wore a rumpled lightweight blue suit and green bow tie. With black polka dots. Was it the tie which scared everyone off?

"You don't seem to have many candidates at this table," said Robert.

Mr. Bow-tie, a small man with thinning hair and walnut-colored plastic-framed glasses, hands folded neatly in front of him, smiled pleasantly. "Not at the moment, no. You're the first."

"I have to ask. Are you related to Mr. Rogers?"

A gentle laugh. "I'm a fan; my three children were raised listening to him, but I can't say we're personally acquainted."

"So tell me," said Robert. "What does BPMA stand for?"

Mr. Bow Tie stuck out his hand. "Horace Wingate. I'm the Director."

"Robert Fairweather."

"And BPMA stands for the Bureau of Program and Management Analysis."

"What does that mean, exactly?"

"First, the context. We're the agency that supervises all housing in New York City outside that of the Housing Authority. It's divided into three major offices: Property Management, Development, and Rent and Housing Maintenance. BPMA is a small unit reporting directly to the Commissioner and what we're responsible for is examining each of these offices to see if they're doing a good job and to make suggestions for how they can be improved."

"Really? You look at each to see if you can find ways to improve how they do their jobs? And suggest alternatives?"

"You got it."

Robert pondered a moment. "Huh! That actually sounds interesting," he said. "I'm surprised. Analyzing things is something I enjoy. I'm an ex-college professor but right now I'm editing a newspaper in Clinton sponsored by the non-profit PCH. It's a CETA grant and doesn't pay much, but it's also about housing."

"I know the outfit. Millicent Millipede runs it."

"That's right. You know her?"

"Only by reputation."

Robert looked away a moment. "Trying to find a better way of doing things, hmm? This actually sounds like something I could enjoy! And you're the very first person in this whole swarming gathering I've talked to! Imagine that."

"I made a point of finding your resume, Mr. Fairweather. *Dr.* Fairweather, isn't it? I also felt it might be a good fit. If you're still interested by the end of the day, and I haven't hired anyone else, the position is yours."

Robert looked surprised. "Really? That quick? Wow." He cast his eyes around the room. "I . . . uh . . . I guess I should look at a few more places before I decide for good, right?"

"Of course. It's up to you."

"The job pays $16,000 a year, right?"

"Same for everybody here. All these candidates are those who've passed the Staff Analyst's exam. That's the entry wage. No matter which City Department. Later on, raises are possible."

Robert thanked Mr. Wingate and left his table to check out others. Ten minutes later he was back. "I don't think I need any more time. I'm interested."

Wingate smiled. "Looking forward to it." They shook hands again. "You'll report to our Personnel Department. I'll have them send you a start-date in the mail. The address will be on it."

"Just like that?"

"Just like that."

They shook hands once more. And he left with a feeling of lightness. He would soon be earning $6,000 more than he was making now. And the job actually sounded interesting. Who could believe it? It seemed like a miracle.

The Board of *The Clinton Newspaper*, at the meeting following his and Sheila's contretemps at the printer's, upheld Robert's decision, largely because the advisor, Ray Dunleavy (whom Robert had filled in by telephone in advance of the meeting) solidly backed up Robert's position at the printer's. Robert had taken a course from Ray at the very beginning of this job, a course in community newsletters, and when he realized the depth of Dunleavy's experience in journalism, asked him to become the advisor to the newspaper. He was both relieved and pleased when Ray backed up his stand at the printer's, even though there had never been much doubt in his mind that he would.

Although Robert was to stay on and prepare one more issue before he left PCH, he was walking on air when his call to report for duty at the NYC Personnel Department of the Office of Housing came through. Since he'd long ago informed Millicent what was in the offing, she'd had adequate time to look around for a replacement for the second year of the contract. She gave him a big hug and wished him well.

But the best hug, a week or so later, was from Serena on his last official day of work for PCH.

"I will miss you, Robert," she said. "You've been a good friend. And a very understanding one. I'll miss you but at the same time, I'm happy for you. Stay in touch."

"Call me when your man shows up in the States," he said. "So I can meet him and decide whether to shake his hand or punch him in the face."

She smiled. "Go now," she said. "Stay cool, my friend."

And there it was.

Robert stood at the intersection of Fulton and Gold Streets in lower Manhattan. This was, in many ways, the center of power in New York City. It was where the Mayor's

Office was, and City Hall, and Wall Street. But what he was looking at, down Gold only a couple of blocks, was the headquarters of the Department of Housing. He took a moment to gather his feelings. It was like he'd been swimming through a vast and troubled ocean, tiring often but somehow managing to struggle onward, and here, at last, was dry land, the desert island where he'd pulled himself ashore. He had survived to reach it, and he could see in the distance the ship coming to rescue him. He squared his shoulders and took a deep breath.

Suddenly beside him there materialized the small man with the bowtie who had hired him, apparently just out of the subway himself. The tie was maroon this time, with diagonal black stripes.

"Nervous on your first day?" asked Mr. Bow Tie.

"I guess. Yes, a bit. It feels like a big step."

"It will be fine," his boss said. "You'll be fine. The sun is shining. There's no rain. Relax and enjoy it. Let's walk there together."

And they did.

THE END

ACKNOWLEDGEMENTS

Ben Fountain, the author of several best-selling and award-winning books, is an author whose writing workshop I attended in Belize many years ago, and who remains a mentor and friend to this day. Thanks also to novelist and short story writer Jim Shephard; I was fortunate to be part of his *One Story* Sirenland class in Positano, Italy, and I remain a grateful admirer of both him and his work to this day. Scott Sommer, who died years ago unexpectedly and much too soon, was the earliest writer whose classes I attended (at the YMCA in New York City). I would further like to acknowledge the exceptional writer, Grace Paley, regrettably long deceased, whom I met at a literary event in Greenwich Village in New York City years ago and who, after I persuaded her while in a chow line to read a short story of mine, unexpectedly phoned me only a few days later to say: "*Use my name.*"

Further thanks are owed to the late Ronald Story, a retired Professor of History at UMass/Amherst, who passed away in 2024 during a sudden bout with cancer. Ron was amazing, a valued critic as well as the author of several well-regarded works on American History. Though not a relative as far as we'd been able to discover, the fact that he was born in Texas and I in the adjoining state of Oklahoma often caused us to wonder from time to time. Ron and his wife Laura Ricard—also a writer—became dear, dear friends to my partner Jill Hochberg and me, and were immensely encouraging to my writing. I can still close my eyes and recall Ron's chuckle when he read some of the stories in this book.

Quite needless to say—I am indebted to Jill, who not only read, edited, critiqued, and suggested new things for the book, but did so with tact, affection and great skill. This book would not be in your hands if it wasn't for her.

Finally—perhaps surprisingly—I hereby salute all the cab drivers, shoe salesmen, typists, leaflet distributors, bartenders, offset printer operators, newspaper editors and yes, even bankers, for their inadvertent yet lasting contributions both to this book and—let's face it—more broadly, to the City of New York!

READING GROUP
DISCUSSION GUIDE

Thank you for selecting *Professor Fairweather Hits the Skids* for your book club or reading group. This section is intended to help enhance your group's discussion of the book after they've completed it.

Professor Robert Fairweather finds himself both promoted and released from his position at Brooklyn Quintessential University (BQU). It is the early 1970s in New York City, and he soon discovers it's a very troubled time for finding jobs in his field. But he needs to eat and keep a roof over his head. And so we follow him as he embarks on his quest!

For discussion

1. What did —"Hits the Skids"—in the book's title suggest to you? Do you think it was apt?

2. Did you think Robert was trying hard enough to find

work? Why or why not? Can you suggest something else he might have done?

3. Did you feel sympathy for him in his mad scramble to stay afloat? What about the choices he made?

4. The author often tries for droll humor in telling this story. Does it work? Were you amused? If so, what were your favorite moments?

5. Which was your favorite episode? What might you have done had you been in Robert's shoes?

6. Robert shared his apartment with a series of people to help him meet his rent. Whom would *you* least like to have had as your roommate? Did you have a favorite?

7. What did you think of Robert's decision, at the end of the book, to accept a job with the City? Was it the right choice? What might you have done had you found yourself in similar circumstances?

8. Did you live through the 1970s or do you know someone who did? If so, how representative do you think Robert's experiences were?

9. Of all Robert's adventures, which was your favorite, and why?

ABOUT THE AUTHOR

Jim Story is a novelist, short-story writer and poet. His well-received novels *Problems of Translation* (2018) and *The Condor's Shadow* (2023) are available in both print and ebook format.

Jim has published short stories, creative nonfiction, reviews and poetry in a variety of literary publications, has been nominated for a Pushcart Prize, won a Best New Writers Award from Poets & Writers, and held a residency at the Edward Albee Center in Montauk, Long Island. His writing has appeared in *Confrontation*, *The Same*, *Karamu*, *Folio*, *Pindeldyboz*, *Helicon*, *Aspen Anthology*, and many other publications. His blog, *Today's Story*, can be found at his website, *jimcstory.com*.

He lives in New York City, where he is completing a book of short stories based principally on his life and that of his parents on a corporation farm in California's San Joaquin Valley.

"a captivating American odyssey" "a fast-paced tale"

—Jonathan Woods, a
ward-winning author of *Bad Juju*
and *A Death in Mexico*

"A ferocious current keeps pulling you along" "the pure magical brilliance of the language"

—Robert Roth,
author of *Health Proxy* and *Book of Pieces*

"[A] haunting.... Steeped in natural beauty and interpersonal connections."

—D. Donovan,
Senior Reviewer, *Midwest Book Review.*

"Jim Story masterfully takes us into the mind of a man you've probably seen on the street, maybe worked with, shared a passing smile. A man on the run from the skeletons in his past. Get to know him. I did and I'll never forget him."

—Celeste Rita Baker,
author of *Back, Belly & Side: True Lies and False Tales*

"When I saw I only had twenty-three pages left to read of Jim Story's novel *The Condor's Shadow* I thought, "Whoa. Take a break. You don't want this to be over so fast." My resolve lasted 20 seconds. A ferocious current keeps pulling you along....."

—ROBERT ROTH,
AUTHOR *HEALTH PROXY* AND *BOOK OF PIECES*

"Jim Story's *The Condor's Shadow* is a captivating American odyssey. ... Written with humor, grace and beauty, the ballad of Travis Mackey tells of his wanderings through the 20th Century agrarian west and northwest. It's a fast-paced tale of a life lived well under difficult circumstances, a slice of Americana as delicious as your mother's homemade apple pie."

—JONATHAN WOODS,
AWARD-WINNING AUTHOR OF *BAD JUJU*,
A DEATH IN MEXICO AND *KISS THE DEVIL GOODNIGHT*.

"The Pacific Northwest comes alive in all its natural splendor as the backdrop for this poignant tale about an enigmatic drifter who ambles in and out of sleepy no-where towns dodging trouble, but discovers no matter how far he travels, his past is waiting in front of him."

—EVA LESKO NATIELLO,
NEW YORK TIMES BESTSELLING AUTHOR
OF *THE MEMORY BOX*.

"Jim Story again proves to be a master storyteller. In a deeply introspective tale...[and] a story of self-discovery, the novel is also a fine example of nature writing....Another remarkable feature...is the focus on small-town America... specifically the rural communities of the Far West."

—MANUEL G. GONZALES,
AUTHOR OF *MEXICANOS: A HISTORY OF MEXICANS IN THE UNITED STATES*

"*The Condor's Shadow*, Jim Story's new novel, threads scenes like a Native American necklace, each skillfully worked bead different, yet bound together by a common theme.... Read this engrossing Odyssey through the American Northwest to find the answer."

—BOB BACHNER,
AUTHOR OF *LAST CLEAR CHANCE* AND
THE FORTHCOMING *BABY GRAND.*

"This is an engrossing story, cleverly woven—a hero's journey from an embattled youth to a hard-won maturity steeped in sorrow and acceptance."

—HILARY ORBACH,
AUTHOR OF *TRANSGRESSIONS AND OTHER STORIES*

"Part mystery, part suspense with a dash of romance, this compelling, poignant, yet ultimately hopeful novel tells the story of how a single violent event in a young man's life forces him, unfairly, to live his next eighteen years as a fugitive…until fate ultimately leads him to a place of redemption, acceptance, and love."

—CATHIE BORRIE,
AUTHOR OF *THE LONG HELLO: MEMORY,
MY MOTHER, AND ME*

"A brilliant illustration of a moral man's battle with evil and his journey to recall his essential goodness."

—STEPHANIE LATERZA,
AUTHOR OF *THE PSYCHE TRIALS*

"What a marvelous piece of work---a genuine American saga that sweeps us through history before we know it, and a new take on the legend of the loner in the Great West with one of the most decent heroes in a long time…. thoroughly masculine, but in a positive way. ….Everyman in the way we would want him, and ourselves, to be…."

—RONALD STORY (NO RELATION TO JIM),
AUTHOR OF *JONATHAN EDWARDS AND THE GOSPEL OF LOVE*

PROBLEMS OF TRANSLATION
OR
CHARLIE'S COMIC, TERRIFYING, ROMANTIC, LOOPY ROUND-THE-WORLD JOURNEY IN SEARCH OF LINGUISTIC HAPPINESS

Charles Abel Baker sets off around the world to see one of his short stories translated into ten different languages and back again into English. Who knew that literary translation could be so perilous? So romantic? So downright funny?

"An insanely amusing adventure that has a deep love of language at its belly-shaking core."

—GARY SHTEYNGART,
AUTHOR OF *LITTLE FAILURE*, *A SUPER SAD TRUE LOVE STORY*, AND *OUR COUNTRY FRIENDS*

"...A merry yearlong chase around the globe...There is more, much more, and it moves fast. [Jim] Story is impressively inventive, and... adept at the quick surprise and the odd plot twist."

—*KIRKUS REVIEWS*

"...a zany and surprisingly philosophical adventure... One part midlife crisis, one part old-timey spy film, and one part romance, ...a multilayered story that readers... will enjoy." (4/4 Stars)

—*PORTLAND BOOK REVIEW*

"It kept a smile on my face from beginning to end. Suspend disbelief and enjoy the ride!"

— EVA LESKO NATIELLO,
NEW YORK TIMES BESTSELLING AUTHOR OF
THE MEMORY BOX AND *FOLLOWING YOU*

"An incredible wild ride around the world. Intense and fun and hilarious, all. A great read.

— ROBIN McLEAN,
AUTHOR OF *REPTILE HOUSE,*
PITY THE BEAST, AND
GET 'EM YOUNG, TREAT 'EM TOUGH, TELL 'EM NOTHING

Second Edition September 2021
by Indies United Publishing House, LLC

Cover design by Damonza

ISBN 978-1-64456-359-5 [paperback]
ISBN 978-1-64456-360-1 [Mobi]
ISBN 978-1-64456-361-8 [ePub]

Library of Congress Control Number: 2021943117

INDIES UNITED PUBLISHING HOUSE, LLC
P.O. BOX 3071
QUINCY, IL 62305-3071
www.indiesunited.net

To the Rufe's, from one of your orphans.
Thanks for the safe place.